Didn't Like

"Men.

Nate could
the good sense to keep that sentiment to himself.
Besides, he couldn't help but be impressed by
Allie MacLord. She didn't back down when
challenged. "You, uh, have any unmarried female
relatives in the forty to fifty age range?" he asked,
remembering his plan to find a wife for his dad.
"Mothers? Aunts?" Any female biologically
related to this termagant would have no problems
keeping Nate's dad under control. Same gene pool,
after all. Same domineering attitude, he figured.

"Unmarried female relatives?" Allie asked. "What
are you talking about?"

"Nothing," he mumbled, and was mortified to feel
a blush creeping up his neck. When was the last
time he'd blushed? Good grief. What was that all
about?

If Nate didn't know himself better, he might
suspect this woman was causing him to think
about marriage—for himself!

Dear Reader,

The summer after my thirteenth birthday, I read my older sister's dog-eared copy of *Wolf and the Dove* by Kathleen E. Woodiwiss and I was hooked. Thousands of romance novels later—I won't say how many years—I'll gladly confess that I'm a romance freak! That's why I am so delighted to become the associate senior editor for the Silhouette Romance line. My goal, as the new manager of Silhouette's longest-running line, is to bring you brand-new, heartwarming love stories every month. As you read each one, I hope you'll share the magic and experience love as it was meant to be.

For instance, if you love reading about rugged cowboys and the feisty heroines who melt their hearts, be sure not to miss Judy Christenberry's *Beauty & the Beastly Rancher* (#1678), the latest title in her FROM THE CIRCLE K series. And share a laugh with the always-entertaining Terry Essig in *Distracting Dad* (#1679).

In the next THE TEXAS BROTHERHOOD title by Patricia Thayer, *Jared's Texas Homecoming* (#1680), a drifter's life changes for good when he offers to marry his nephew's mother. And a secretary's dream comes true when her boss, who has amnesia, thinks they're married, in Judith McWilliams's *Did You Say...Wife?* (#1681).

Don't miss the savvy nanny who moves in on a single dad, in *Married in a Month* (#1682) by Linda Goodnight, or the doctor who learns his ex's little secret, in *Dad Today, Groom Tomorrow* (#1683) by Holly Jacobs.

Enjoy!

Mavis C. Allen
Associate Senior Editor, Silhouette Romance

Please address questions and book requests to:
Silhouette Reader Service
U.S.: 3010 Walden Ave., P.O. Box 1325, Buffalo, NY 14269
Canadian: P.O. Box 609, Fort Erie, Ont. L2A 5X3

Distracting Dad

TERRY ESSIG

SILHOUETTE *Romance*®
Published by Silhouette Books
America's Publisher of Contemporary Romance

For everyone at Silhouette—
thanks for noticing that manuscript
with the crayon drawings on the back all those years ago
and rescuing it from the slush pile,
as well as all the help and guidance since then.
Here comes lucky number thirteen.

 SILHOUETTE BOOKS

ISBN 0-373-19679-2

DISTRACTING DAD

Copyright © 2003 by Mary Therese Essig

Visit Silhouette at www.eHarlequin.com

Printed in U.S.A.

Books by Terry Essig

Silhouette Romance

House Calls #552
The Wedding March #662
Fearless Father #725
Housemates #1015
Hardheaded Woman #1044
Daddy on Board #1114
Mad for the Dad #1198
What the Nursery Needs... #1272
The Baby Magnet #1435
A Gleam in His Eye #1472
Before You Get to Baby... #1583
Distracting Dad #1679

Silhouette Special Edition

Father of the Brood #796

TERRY ESSIG

says that writing is her escape valve from a life that leaves little time for recreation or hobbies. With a husband and six young children, Terry works on her stories a little at a time, between seeing to her children's piano, sax and trombone lessons, their gymnastics, ice skating and swim team practices, and her own activities of leading a Brownie troop, participating in a car pool and attending organic chemistry classes. Her ideas, she says, come from her imagination and her life—neither one of which is lacking!

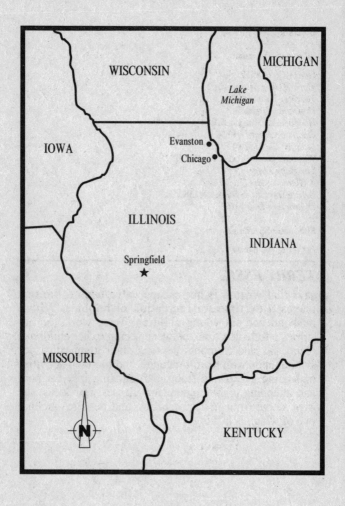

Chapter One

"An older woman. That's what I'm thinking. Widowed, divorced, I'm not in a position to be picky. Or it could be somebody younger with a mother. Everybody has a mother. One of them must be widowed or divorced, you would think."

Nathaniel Edward Parker paused in his speech, leaning back in his chair behind the large wooden desk in his office. Across from him was his longtime best friend and business partner, Jared Hunter. They were supposed to be having a business meeting. Jared looked up from the papers in front of him wearing a very puzzled look on his face. "What? Nate, could you please stay focused here? We need to convince Harry Zigler to sign this contract so we can pay our rent next month."

"Sorry. I'm a little distracted."

"No kidding. Look, buddy, I need you to pay attention. This is important."

"And this isn't? I've got a serious problem here, Jared."

Jared looked disgruntled. "Yeah? Well, you've got another one right here. This contract..."

Nate ruthlessly interrupted Jared. "I cannot pay attention to the contract. God knows I've tried, but it's impossible. Maybe if we clear up this other issue I'll be able to concentrate."

Jared blew out a sigh. "What other issue? We have to make up a list of people we know who have mothers before you can focus? What is that all about?"

"*Available* mothers. Big difference." Nate drummed his desktop with his fingers. "For my dad. Ever since Mom died, he's been making me crazy."

Jared snorted. "So what else is new? Your mom's been dead for two years. You should be used to it by now."

Nate raked a hand through his blond hair. "No. Lately it's been getting worse. I can't concentrate because I keep expecting him to come bursting in here with some other bizarre way we can improve the business."

"Giving away Fourth of July fireworks with the company logo on the package wasn't that bizarre."

"Please. Nobody who saw them blow would realize that blue and green are the company colors and the first person who loses a hand would sue our butts off. You can bet dear old Dad wouldn't offer to pay the lawyer's bill, either. He can't. He doesn't have that kind of money."

Jared rattled the papers on the table. "About this contract," he began determinedly.

Nate flattened his palm over the rustling papers. "Not until I have my list."

Throwing up his hands, Jared relented. "All right, all right. I'm almost afraid to ask. What do you plan to do with this list of people with mothers. *Available* mothers," Jared immediately corrected before Nate could. "Marry the old guy off?"

"Well, yeah."

"You're not serious, are you?" Jared pointed an accusing finger at his buddy. "You *are* serious." He threw himself back in his chair. "Aw, man, I don't believe this. What are we, a dating service now? We've got a business here, Nate. We don't have time to run a lonely hearts club, too."

"Well, we can't take care of business with my father breathing down our necks, now can we? The man is lost without Mom, lost. The way I see it, the only solution we've got is to find him some other interest in life besides me, his only son." Nate sat up, his irritation with his partner's obtuseness obvious.

"A wife, for example?" Jared asked.

"Exactly. Look. It's obvious." Nate picked up a marker and leaned to the side, writing on a large sheet of paper clipped to a tripod. "Look, we'll flowchart it. Try and follow along." He wrote the word *father* in large block type at the top of the paper and pointed to it. "My father."

Jared rolled his eyes and nodded. "Your father."

"Has been sticking his nose in where it doesn't belong, making us crazy on a daily basis since my mom passed away." Nate drew a dash down from the word *father* and wrote *Nate and Jared.*

"I still don't think the fireworks were that bad an idea."

"Shut up. Dad needs something to distract him from us, right?"

Jared nodded. "Okay. Distractions can be good. That would probably work."

"He needs a woman in his life. He never bugged me like this when Mom was around. She kept him occupied."

"I don't mean to speak disrespectfully of the dead, but your mom was nuts," Jared pointed out, stating what he thought to be the obvious. "Keeping her out of trouble was a full-time occupation for your father."

Nate shrugged. It was the truth. "Mom distracted him, see?"

"Uh-huh. So we make this list of available women and this helps us...how? Exactly how do we get them together?" Jared waggled a finger admonishingly. "And no force allowed. Shotgun weddings went out a long time ago."

Nate waggled the marker right back at his partner. "We'll worry about that part when we get that far. Think about it. This makes perfect sense. *Somebody* we know is bound to have an unattached female relative of the right age somewhere in their family tree. We just have to find her. Once we accomplish that, we sic her on Pop. Women are supposed to be naturally nurturing, right? She'll be all over him, cooking him wholesome dinners and stuff like that. He won't be able to resist. She distracts him, see? Then he leaves us alone. Easy."

Openly snickering at his buddy's logic, Jared asked, "Naturally nurturing, huh? I don't know about that. I've been out with one or two that would probably eat their own young." But he gave it some thought. "You, um, really think this will work?"

Nate reached for the coffeepot that sat on a warmer on one side of the table. "Damn straight."

Jared held out his coffee cup. "Okay, if you say so. Now, who goes on the list? And don't say my mother. I don't want her tangled in your nutty schemes. Then she'd start driving me crazy."

Nate took a cautious sip of hot coffee. "No, your mother's out. I'll admit I thought about her, but I don't think she'd put up with my father's antics. Doesn't she have any unmarried sisters or anything?"

"No."

"Not even one?"

"No. God broke the mold after creating my mother."
Jared folded his hands together and raised his eyes piously.
"Thank you, God."

Nate slumped in his chair. "Okay, all right. Who do we
know who does?"

The two men sat, marking the highly polished conference
tabletop with fingerprints as they drummed their fingers and
thought.

Tentatively Jared offered out loud, "Anne Reid brought
in brownies the other day. She must have a mother."

Nate snorted. "They were awful. Her mother probably
taught her everything she doesn't know about baking and
Dad's an old-fashioned kind of guy. He'd never go for a
woman who couldn't bake."

"All right, I tried. This is your problem, you think of
somebody."

"Our problem," Nate corrected. "Remember the contract? I can't concentrate until we take care of this." Nate
gave Jared a mean little smile. "And just so you know,
Dad's signed up for a computer class over at the high
school's adult education program. He's decided to help us
with our books."

Jared unstacked his feet and sat up straight, suddenly far
more serious. "Fine. Mitzi Malone."

"She was hatched, not born. Try again."

The phone rang. Both men looked at it, then at each
other. "You get it. If it's my father, I'm not here."

"You get it. It's probably my mother."

"Could be Sue Ann calling to tell you she can't live
without you. What if it's a client?"

"They'll leave a message."

The machine did, in fact, pick up. Nate and Jared's argument was broken into by a vivacious female voice. "Mr.
Parker, this is Allison MacLord. I live in the condo just

below yours? Please call me as soon as you get this message. There's something leaking from your place down into mine. You've got a broken pipe or something. My bed's soaked. I think you may have ruined my ceiling. Oh, ick, the carpet's all squishy. You have insurance, right? My number's 27…''

Nate snatched up the phone, and yelled into it, ''What are you talking about Miss…whatever you said your name was? What's leaking?''

Allison Marie MacLord held the phone away from her ear and blinked at it. One minute she'd been talking to a machine and the next a very vital, very vibrant, very forceful male voice. ''Well, um, I don't exactly know, Mr. Parker. I mean I just got home. My ceiling's dripping, some paint's already peeled and fallen, my mattress may never dry out and water's welling up every time I take a step on the bedroom carpet. My feet are getting wet right through my shoes, which really makes me mad because I paid ten dollars for that water protecting spray they're always trying to sell you at the shoe stores.''

Nate swore.

On her end, Allie grimaced. She hated confrontation. When the answering machine had picked up, she'd been almost relieved, except for the fact that leaving a message wasn't going to stop the steady flow of…whatever anytime soon. ''Mr. Parker? You are 3H, aren't you? That's what the mailbox says. Your next-door neighbor thought this was where you worked.''

Nate put his hand over the phone's receiver. ''Dad insisted my garbage disposal wasn't working right the other night. God only knows what he did while he was crawling around under my sink.'' He lifted his hand and spoke into the phone. ''3H, yeah, that's me. Damn it.''

''Um…'' Allie sighed. This wasn't going at all well.

"Ah, I don't suppose anyone around here has a spare key to your place?"

Nate dropped his head into his hand. "No. No spare keys."

"You really should leave one with a neighbor, you know. What if you lock yourself out sometime? Then what would you do?"

"Miss M—"

"Allie. You should probably call me Allie. You did just destroy my bed, after all. You know, if you'd left a spare with a neighbor I could go in there for you and try to figure out what the problem is. Maybe call a plumber."

Nate sighed. "What color is it?"

"What?"

"The…whatever that is dripping."

"Oh." Allie's gaze drifted up. "It is, uh, kind of a very light brown." It could be water simply picking up color as it passed through the beams over her head, but it could be something else totally. Yuck. "Ah, it seems to be picking up speed. I don't know how much more my bed and carpet can absorb. If we don't hurry here, it's going to go down to the ceiling in 1H below me. If it hasn't already—"

Nate swore again. "I'm on my way." He threw down the phone and stood. "I've got to go. My father is single-handedly destroying my entire building and something tells me he doesn't carry workman's insurance."

Jared had the low class to laugh. "Better hurry, man." He quickly grew serious. God only knows what havoc the old guy could wreak on their books. "Meanwhile, I'll keep thinking."

"Thanks, man." Nate glowered as he raced out the door.

Slamming the car door as he jumped into his car did nothing but make the hand he caught in it hurt, and the speeding ticket he collected on the way cost him valuable time. By the time he reached his building, Nate was fuming. Still he pulled cautiously into a parking slot lest he somehow overshoot the space and smack right into the side of the building. If bad luck came in threes, he'd met his quota for the day. But there was no point in pushing his karma or whatever. One thing for sure, Nate was not meeting with any clients or signing any contracts today. Climbing out of the car, he closed the door without slamming it and hurried into the building. Not willing to wait for the elevator, he took the stairs two at a time. He juggled his keys in his palm as he made his way down the hall, then took a fortifying breath before opening the door to 3H. Cautiously Nate peaked in.

"Hell," he said to no one in particular, and followed it up with something more pungent.

The living room carpet he stepped onto was dry. But he could see that water came to within a few inches of its border. Gingerly he made his way across the island of the living room to stare at the flooded kitchen. In the center of the room the water appeared to be over an inch deep. That was obviously the low spot created when the building settled. With a distasteful expression on his face, Nate toed off his good shoes. He leaned down to pull off his dark socks and roll up his pant legs. He waded in.

"Like I don't have enough problems," he muttered as he slogged his way over to the sink. "Economy's nuts, dot coms dropping like no tomorrow." He pulled open the cabinet door below the sink and squatted down to peer at a spaghetti bowl of pipes he would have preferred never getting to know on such an intimate basis.

"Not only do I have to put up with Dad's business advice and dire warnings on the economy but now he's got to turn into Handyman Negri's evil counterpart. Unhandyman Ted runs amok. Again. Damn it, Dad, what did you

do under here last night? I swear to God it's the last time
I invite you to dinner because I feel bad about you eating
alone. *I* eat alone practically every night and *I* survive.''
Tentatively Nate reached out and touched an alien-looking
length of white PVC pipe.

The phone rang.

Nate jumped and cracked his head on the underside of
the counter.

''Ouch! Damn it!''

He backed out from under the sink, grabbed one of the
kitchen towels his last girlfriend had bought him—see?
women worried about stuff like that—swiped it over his
hands and nabbed the telephone. ''What,'' he growled.
''Make it good. This is not turning out to be one of my
better days.''

''Um, Mr. Parker?''

Nate sighed. It was that Allison person. The one whose
apartment his father had ruined. Nate struggled for a bit of
sympathy, but honestly, it was tough to find when he was
standing in the swamp that used to be his kitchen. ''Yes?''
It was all he could manage with any degree of civility.

''This is Allie MacLord. 2H?''

Nate rubbed tiredly at his forehead, took the portable
phone with him as he ducked back down to peer under the
sink again. ''Ms. MacLord, I just—''

''Allie.''

Nate rubbed his forehead harder and dutifully repeated,
''Allie. Look, I just walked in the door. I haven't really
had time to—''

''Oh, my timing is perfect then. I'll be right up to help.
My place won't dry out until you quit dripping into it, you
know.''

''I know—'' He stepped, realizing he was talking to a
dead phone. The woman had hung up on him. He, Mr.

Masters in Business Administration, hadn't managed to finish one sentence during their entire conversation. Now she was on her way up to finish off his ego by watching what a nonstarter he was with plumbing issues. "Real men know how, where and when to use a pipe wrench," he told himself as he poked the end button on the phone and reached above his head to set the receiver on the counter.

Nate didn't even own a pipe wrench.

He comforted himself. "Like I was saying earlier, the apple doesn't fall all that far from the tree. It's pretty obvious to me that Dad's not all that hot with a wrench, either. At least I'm man enough to admit I don't know what I don't know." It wasn't all that much comfort as water continued to gush.

The doorbell sang out Allie's arrival. "God help me," he muttered as he closed his eyes in silent resignation. Nate called out, "Come in. It's not locked."

Nate heard the door open, then close. Seconds later a feminine voice said, "Oh, my."

Not exactly the response that had come first to his mind upon viewing the scene, but hey, everyone was different. "Yeah," he said. "Goll darn. What a mess." He looked back over his shoulder and about fell on his butt into the water.

Allison, oops Allie MacWhoever was a pixie. A sprite. Nate bet she was a foot shorter than his own six foot two and if she turned around, he believed he'd see fairy wings. She was slightly built and, he'd bet his last dot com, Irish. Or Scottish. One or the other. Her hair was deep red verging on auburn. It was cut short and framed her face in soft waves. Her eyes were a clear, brilliant emerald-green and, even from across the room, he could see the freckles marching across the bridge of her nose, not because the freckles were so large or dark; they weren't, but because her skin was so milky pale anything would stand out in contrast.

She stood on tiptoe at the edge of the floodplain, her hands tucked into the front pockets of stone-colored shorts that rode below on her hipbone. Her pink tank top barely met the top of her shorts and when she moved, as in breathed, a tantalizing narrow band of belly peaked out. For a short person, she had amazingly long legs. They were slim yet shapely and ended in little elf feet sporting amazingly pink flip-flops with orange and pink silk floppy flowers growing from the vamp.

Damn, but she was cute. Not pretty. Cute.

But cute could be good.

All Nate's manly protective instincts went on red alert and he scowled. Who had let this little baby doll loose on her own in the world? What kind of parents did she have that they'd let a maybe eighteen-year-old alone with nobody to watch out for her? Morons. This Allie had morons for parents.

Allie gave Nathaniel Parker an odd look as she kicked off her flip-flops and prepared to wade in. The guy looked like he was in a trance or something. What was he staring at? Self-consciously she rubbed along her upper lip, feeling for remnants of the *pb* and *j* she'd scarfed down while waiting for some sign of life up above her, but she didn't feel anything.

"Are you okay?" she asked, moving closer.

"What?" Nate shook his head to clear his brain and put a hand down in the water to help with his balance. "Sorry. I just—spaced out there for a moment, I guess."

Allie splashed her way over to squat next to Nate. "What have we got?"

"A problem. A real problem. See this pipe here?" Nate gestured to the culprit pipe that was spurting water down under the sink. "It's broken. My father must have bumped it and loosened it last night when he was playing around with the garbage disposal. See how close it is to the disposal? Pressure must have built up during the day until it burst."

"Yeah, looks like," Allie agreed, looking at Nate expectantly.

"Yeah." Nate nodded solemnly. "Looks like."

"You going to fix it?"

"Um. Well. Where's the water turnoff in your place?"

Allie reached past him and turned a knob. "Right here." The flow slowed to a trickle.

Nate moved her hand aside and tightened the knob farther. The water shut off completely. "Great. Now let's see. I guess I need a wrench or something."

"Call a plumber," Allie advised. "Where's your mop?"

"No, look. See? If we just align these two ends again and give this thing a couple of twists—"

"What is it with men? You can't ask for directions even if you have no idea where you are. You can't admit when you're in over your head with a home repair. What is wrong with calling in a professional? Look at this mess!" Allie made a wide sweep with her hand and Nate had to lean backward to avoid being hit.

"It would have taken a plumber one third the time and I'd have a bed to sleep in tonight if you and your father hadn't decided to play handyman last night."

Nate puffed up with indignation over that. He'd practically ordered his father to leave his plumbing alone last night. This was not his fault. The blame lay squarely with his dad. "Now just hang on a second—"

But he never got to finish his sentence.

Allie rose in disgust. "Men. What was God thinking of?"

He could ask the same about women, Nate thought, but had the good sense to keep the sentiment to himself. "Look—"

"And where's the darn mop? There's no point in even starting on my place until yours is taken care of. It's just going to keep dripping down otherwise."

You had to be impressed. He towered over her, yet she didn't back away. It was as if Allie didn't even notice the size difference. Nate opened his pantry door and got out a mop. "You, uh, have any unmarried female relatives in the forty-to-fifty age range?" he asked as he began sopping up water. "Mother? Aunts?" Any female biologically related to this termagant would have no problems keeping his dad under control. Nate would bet the business on it. Same gene pool, after all. Same domineering attitude, he figured.

Allie had gone into the bathroom to raid his clothes hamper. She had several dirty bath towels in her hands, which she threw on the floor. "Unmarried female relatives? What are you talking about?"

Nate squeezed out the mop over the bucket he'd retrieved. "Nothing," he mumbled, and was mortified to feel a blush creeping up his neck. When was the last time he'd blushed? Good grief. His father had him so crazed, he wasn't even filtering his thoughts. They were simply entering his head and exiting his mouth. "Nothing at all."

Allie gave him a suspicious look before picking up a sodden towel and twisting it over the bucket. "You need to do your laundry," she said. "Your hamper's full."

"I know," he replied humbly, not willing to argue with the termagant. She was on a roll and with good reason, Nate grudgingly admitted to himself. He had ruined her apartment, after all, which meant that when he finished his own lengthy cleanup, he'd be only half-done. With that thought, Nate excused himself and called his father.

"Pop, get over here," he said into the receiver. "*We've* got a problem." He stressed the plural pronoun. "And there's somebody you've got to meet."

The senior Mr. Parker showed up in time to watch the last bucket of water being dumped down the toilet. He entered the condo with windblown hair and a lot of grumbling over the abrupt summons. He'd been studying his computer manual, he groused. Had just started getting the hang of those little icon things and what the heck was so all-fired important?

Nate had gotten his blue eyes from his father, Allie noticed. And probably his hair color as well, though it was hard to tell from the older man's graying crop. Allie would guess Nate to be in his late twenties to early thirties, which meant his father was at least somewhere over the midcentury mark. The man had aged well. Physically fit with broad shoulders and relatively flat stomach, Nate's dad still had all his hair, excellent posture and only faint crow's-feet extending from the corners of his eyes. If Nate took after his father, his wife would have no complaints thirty-odd years down the road.

His dad's handshake was firm when Allie stuck out her hand. "How do you do, sir?"

"Ted," Nate's father corrected. "Call me Ted. And I do fine." He frowned at his son. "Most of the time. When this one's not giving me ulcers."

If anybody was giving anyone ulcers, Nate thought irritably, his dad was doing Nate's stomach lining in, not the other way around. "Your timing is impeccable, Dad," Nate said. "The dirty work is over."

Allie frowned. "Don't forget about my place."

Nate smiled painfully. "Right. How could I?" He sighed. "Dad, you take the clothes basket down to the laundry room and get a load of towels started, will you? There are quarters in my top bureau drawer. I need to go downstairs and see how bad Allie's condo is.''

But his father wouldn't hear of it. ''No, I'll go. I caused the problem, I guess, although I can't believe it since I didn't touch the pipes. I only worked on the garbage disposal, which is not leaking, from what I understand.''

Nate rolled his eyes. The pipes were only right *next* to the garbage disposal.

''Still, I'll check out Allie's place. You go ahead and get your laundry taken care of. Allie and I will be just fine.'' With that pronouncement, Ted took Allie's arm to lead her out of the condo. ''So, my dear, how old are you?''

''Twenty-eight, Ted.''

Nate narrowly missed dropping the heavily laden hamper on his foot. Twenty-eight? No way. He thought he'd been generous with a guess of eighteen.

''Really?'' he heard his father say. ''My, my, getting up there. Any boyfriends? Serious ones, that is. Little thing like you could use a man to look after her, right?''

''Actually I'm quite capable of looking after myself.'' Allie glowered over her shoulder at Nate. ''That is, unless some big strapping male with nothing better to do with his time decides to flood my condo.''

Nate immediately pointed the finger at his father. ''Hey, don't look at me. This was his doing, every bit of it. Everything was working fine until he stuck his nose under my sink.''

Allie arched an eyebrow. ''Aren't you a little old to be passing the buck?'' she inquired.

''I am not passing the buck,'' Nate said. ''It's the truth.'' He waved a frustrated hand in an erasing motion. ''Oh, never mind. It doesn't matter. Just go down and show my father the mess, will you? I'll get this load started and be right there.''

''You shouldn't leave your clothes in the laundry room,'' Allie informed him. ''Someone might steal them.''

''Out of a working machine?''

She nodded. ''Yes. It happened to me in my college dorm.''

Oh, yeah? And what was her degree in? Mother henism? Writing advice columns? ''I'll chance it,'' Nate said with a forced smile. ''You've got enough problems,'' he advised her. ''You really shouldn't worry your pretty little head over mine.'' He smiled condescendingly, knowing he'd just gotten her goat but good.

''Wouldn't think of it,'' she said. ''Just don't knock on my door when you need a towel so you can take your shower.''

''Wouldn't think of it,'' Nate responded just as insincerely. He rolled his eyes and took off for the laundry room before this ridiculous nonconversation went any further.

Nate dumped soap into the bottom of a couple of washing machines then started tossing lights into one, darks into the other in a rather haphazard fashion. He only shrugged when he noticed a dark sock had gotten in with his underwear, not bothering to retrieve it.

''All right, so I wrecked her bed, her ceiling and quite possibly her floor,'' Nate muttered to himself as he gave the controls a vicious twist. ''I said I'd take care of it, didn't I?'' Nate's stomach clutched at the sound of water running into the machines. He ran his palm over his abdomen soothing it. ''Just like a woman. Get a hold of something and never let it go. Probably thinks I won't make good on it,'' he continued to mutter as he stacked the detergent box into the empty clothes hamper. ''Well, she doesn't need to

worry. When Nathaniel Parker says he's going to take care
of something, it's as good as done.''

Self-righteously he picked up his supplies and, with one
final baleful glare at the filling machines, turned away. ''I'll
tell you what, anybody takes anything out of those machines before I get back and that woman gets to say I told
you so, they're dead meat. Dead meat,'' he repeated, almost
wishing someone would try. He was in the mood to take
somebody on, no doubt about that.

Nate bounded back up the stairs. He dropped his hamper
off at his place, grabbed the mop and bucket and headed
down to 2H. No point in putting off the agony.

The door to Allie's condo wasn't closed tightly and Nate
nudged it open with his foot as his hands were full.

''Yes, well it's like I was saying, my son seems to be
having trouble finding himself a good woman, Allie.
Course, he's looking in all the wrong places. Singles bars.''
Ted made a disgusted sound. ''What do you get when you
pick up somebody at a bar? An alcoholic, that's what. A
good woman doesn't hang out in a bar, for God's sake.''

Nate had obviously caught the end of a conversation.
Sad, sorrowful and deep, that was definitely his dad and,
unless Nate missed his guess, dear old dad was on another
one of his rolls, with Nate once again the topic of choice.

''And a man needs a good woman. A wife can make or
break a man,'' Ted continued to expound. ''God knows
I've tried explaining that simple concept over and over, but
Nate just doesn't seem to get it. I don't suppose, since you
don't have anyone special…no? Well, maybe you have a
friend?''

Nate dropped the bucket on his foot.

He couldn't believe it. His father was sneaking around

behind his back trying to marry him off! If that wasn't the most underhanded, conniving, manipulative thing the old man had tried yet, Nate didn't know what was.

And besides, he'd thought of it first.

Chapter Two

With the sound of the clattering bucket, two heads poked into the room. "Wha—oh, uh, Nate, you get your laundry started already?"

Nate righted the bucket, then stood up and looked at his father. "Yeah, Dad, I did. Can I talk to you for a moment?" Nate gestured to the open condo door. "Out in the hallway maybe?"

Ted cleared his throat. "Well now, nothing I'd rather do than have a heart-to-heart with my one and only son, don't you know. But little Allie here was showing me her bedroom. I gotta tell you, son, it's a mess. Yes, indeed." Ted pointed behind him. "I'm afraid our little talk will have to take a back seat. Here, have a look at this."

Nate shook his head in disparagement. No way was his father getting away with this. "Dad—"

"No, really, come have a look."

Nate heaved a great sigh and pushed away from the mop and bucket. He could hold his own with the CFO of any major corporation, but with his own father, he was clueless as how to proceed. "Fine, Dad. Let's see. Show me the mess."

Allie's condo appeared to be laid out exactly the same as his own, only reversed. But the décor screamed female in the house. They ought to get one of those decorator magazine editors in here, Nate decided as he reluctantly wound his way through the small foyer, to the efficiency kitchen, and on into the living-dining area and then the bedroom.

Nate took a last look around. Yeah, some editor could do a great series on how the same layout could look totally different with just a few changes in paint and furniture. Nate liked to think of his own place as, well, masculine. Little wonder, as it just so happened his condo was full of what Nate considered manly stuff. Guy choices. Tan carpet, brown leather sofa pit, modern pictures loaded with these really cool geometric shapes in tan, brown and black that didn't try to be anything other than what they were: cool shapes. There wasn't a candle in the place, no overburdened silk flower arrangements and definitely no little artsy-fartsy ceramic bowls brimming with stinky potpourri sitting around catching dust, making you sneeze. And pink? What was that? Certainly not a color in Nate's vocabulary.

Allie's place couldn't be more girly girl. Pink might not be the only word in her vocabulary but it was darn close. And knickknacks? Good grief, the woman could open a store. She could stock it for a year out of her living room alone. Nate sniffed in dismissal, turned around and looked up at the bedroom ceiling.

Oh, God. He needed to check his insurance policy. The problem was, he knew he'd taken a high deductible to lower the rates. He hoped to heaven this type of thing was covered, because he suspected he'd exceeded even his exorbitant deductible.

"Holy cow."

"Yes," his father agreed. "It's a mess all right." He slapped Nate on the back. "Well, we've got our work cut out for us, son."

Nate, his father and Allie watched as a drop of water fell from the stained ceiling and hit the bed with a sodden plop.

Ted scratched his head. "Probably take a while for the water that was already trapped between your floor and her ceiling to work its way through now that we've stopped the leak. I hope it doesn't drip too much longer, though. The carpet's pretty well saturated already. Know anybody with a wet vac?"

Allie volunteered to ring neighbors' doorbells while Nate and Ted wrestled the mattress off the bed.

As they struggled to guide their sodden burden through the bedroom doorway, Nate mused that it wasn't so much the mattress he minded replacing, it was the bed linens themselves. This room too was done in early Easter egg. Come on, pink and yellow and wimpy purple—no, lavender—that was what you called washed-out purple, lavender. Nate decided then and there to just give her the money. She'd have to replace the stuff herself. No way was he going to go into a store and buy pale purple anything. From the looks of things, this Allie woman didn't have many guys staying over, that was for sure. No guy would sleep in a bed done up like a flower bower. And it smelled...girly in here. Wet, but still girly. Nate sniffed deeply and told himself he didn't like it.

Ted looked back up to the ceiling as he helped Nate shove the box spring out of the room, and Nate's eyes followed.

They watched another drop work its way loose from its moorings and do a free fall. Nate winced.

"Hey, look what I've got," Allie called as she appeared

in the doorway pushing what appeared to be a giant, lethal-looking vacuum cleaner. "A wet vac. Cool, huh? Mrs. Naderly had one. She said the basement in the house she used to live in before she scaled down to an apartment used to get water. She also has some floor fans to help dry things further after we suck up as much as we can out of the carpet."

Nate gave her a halfhearted smile. "Great. That's just really…great."

Ted slung companionable arms around his son and Allie as though they were the best of buddies. "Tell you what. Let's handle the carpet as best we can and then while we're waiting for things to dry up some, why don't we head to the hardware store? We can pick up what we need to repair the ceiling. If the seams in the drywall start to pop as it dries, we'll be ready. Get little Allie here taken care of in no time."

"I really think it might be better if we called in a professional, Ted," Allie said.

"Dad, since when do you know how to repair plaster?"

"No need to bother some busy construction company when we can take care of this ourselves," Ted insisted. "They'd never come for something so little, anyway. And how hard can it be?" He gestured toward the ceiling. "It's not even real plaster, just that drywall stuff. Hell, we'll go buy a can of that gunk you use, the kind that's all premixed, and slap some up there. Have the whole thing back to normal in nothing flat. You'll see."

"Oh, God. Where have I heard those words before?" Nate asked the heavens.

His father turned on him. "I still say this has nothing to do with anything I did last night. It's strictly coincidental that your water pipes decided to introduce you to your neighbor the day after I worked on the garbage disposal."

"Yeah, right. Whatever."

"It's true," Ted insisted.

Nate put his hand up in a "hold it" gesture. "Look, the how is no longer important. The situation exists. Let's call a plasterer, let him deal with this and I'll take you both out to dinner. What do you say?"

All Ted had to say was a chiding "Nate—"

Nate turned away from his father while he ground his teeth together. Then he spun back around to face him once more. "Dad, you really need to go back to work. Early retirement was a mistake. You need a life outside of—" Nate gestured up "—making me crazy doing this kind of thing."

Ted shook a finger at him. "No. No, you're wrong. All those years I concentrated on my career and for what? I missed my son's childhood, my wife became a virtual stranger. She pulled all kinds of antics just to be noticed, is my guess. Then when I realized what had happened, arranged things so we could get to know each other again, it was too late. Your mom passed away." Ted punctuated his words with vehement arm and hand gesticulations. "Well, I've learned my lesson and I'm telling you, this is what's important. My son and the things that affect his happiness. You're all I've got left. You may be a man now, Nate, but I'm still your father. And you know what they say."

Nate gritted his teeth. "No, Dad, what do they say?"

"Better late than never, that's what. I may not have always been there for you when you were a kid, but I've turned over a new leaf, learned my lesson. You can count on me. I'll be here for you from now on. That's a promise you can take to the bank."

That's just what Nate was afraid of.

"Now here's what we're going to do. We'll go to the

hardware store and then the Sleep Factory. After that, you'll
take Allie and me out to dinner, okay?''

Nate clenched and unclenched his hands several times in
frustration. His father really seemed to believe that making
him crazy was in reality a way of a father reaching out to
his son. How could you argue with a guy for trying to bond
with his son? You couldn't. You'd only lose and look like
a heartless jerk in the process. Might as well save some
time and cave right then and there. "Okay, Dad, you win,"
he said, but he didn't like it. "Let's go to the hardware
store."

His father slapped him heartily on the back as Nate gave
a last, disgusted look up at Allie's ceiling. "That's the
spirit, son, that's the spirit."

Nate was pretty sure that Allie had called the situation
earlier. They should just skip over the screwing-everything-
up-royally part and go right to calling in a professional.
Save a lot of time, effort and money. He'd seen his dad in
action before. It wasn't a pretty sight. But now, in an attempt to humor his dad, they were going to take a project
that would take somebody else a day or two, complicate it,
lengthen it and multiply the cost, all by a factor of at least
two. Nate sighed to himself. Well, maybe it would work
out. If he and his dad hung with Allie for a while, they
might meet some of her friends or relatives. An unmarried
older female relative with Allie's spunk might work out
real well here.

Nate commandeered the wet vac and extracted a good
couple of gallons of water from the carpet while Ted and
Allie bagged up her wet sheets, blanket and spread to take
to a Laundromat, which had oversize machines that could
handle the load, the next day. When Nate felt they'd accomplished as much as possible, he called a time-out. "All
right, people, that's it for a while. It's getting late and I'm

hungry. Let's head on out of here.'' Ted beat them all to the door. Nate assumed he was hungry, too.

Allie grabbed her purse as she passed through the kitchen area. She wasn't that hungry, but she didn't want to look at the mess her beautiful condo had become any longer, either. ''Your father is such a sweetheart,'' she said as she locked up.

Nate rolled his eyes. Sweet. Yeah, right. The old sweetheart had just about demolished Allie's apartment. What was that all about? A major cavity caused by all that sweetness? ''Listen, Allie,'' Nate said. ''I know this is going to be a big inconvenience for you, but I'll make it up to you.'' Somehow. ''Dad means well and he really wants to try to fix things up for you. If you'll just let him putz around in there for a while before we call in somebody else, someone who actually knows what they're doing, I swear I'll make it up to you. I don't know how, but I will.''

Allie looked at him askance. ''You're being kind of mean-spirited, don't you think? It's not like he did it on purpose. It was a mistake. What are you, Mr. Perfect? I mean, maybe you don't get along with your father, but you still shouldn't downgrade him like that.''

Nate recoiled. She was attacking *him?* All he was trying to do was correct an error his father had made. Not Nate's error, Ted's. He felt justifiably put-upon. ''Of course, it was a mistake. Nobody would do this kind of thing on purpose, and no I'm not perfect. I'm just saying I've dealt with my father all my life. You haven't. I know what to expect here.'' Chaos. Bedlam. Further disaster.

''He certainly sounds as if he knows what he's doing.''

''Yeah, he does, doesn't he?'' And he'd seen his mother weep real tears over some of the repair jobs Ted had done for her. And they hadn't been tears of gratitude. Nate held up his hands in surrender. ''Okay, fine. Not another word.

We're going to get the taping compound right now,'' Nate informed her. "And then I guess we'll see.''

"Yes, I guess we will.'' And Allie's expression stated more clearly than words who she thought would be getting their eyes opened.

"Come on, children, you're dawdling.''

"Right behind you, Dad.'' Nate lowered his voice once more. "Just don't say I didn't tell you so.'' Nate held up one hand. "Maybe I'll be proved wrong.'' When pigs flew. "I hope I am. Honest, I do. But just in case, here's how we'll play it. We'll let him play around a little bit, you'll tell him what a great job he did—I hope you're a good liar—we'll wait a couple days for him to lose interest and stop checking on it to make sure his repair is holding, which it might, although it'll look like garbage. Once he's satisfied, that's when I'll call in somebody who actually knows what they're doing. You know, a professional.'' Nate held up one hand, palm out. His index and middle fingers were up, his thumb touching his bent fourth and fifth digits in an old scouting gesture of sincerity. His other hand lay on his chest over his heart. He had all bases covered. "I swear. Trust me.''

Allie glared at him. "You are being such a jerk.''

"I just don't want you panicking, that's all.'' And she would. Nate grimaced, thinking of some of his father's home repairs he'd witnessed. Would she ever. "So when the time comes, remember. I promise I'll take care of it.''

Allie rolled her eyes. "Fine. I'll remember.''

"What are you doing over there, reciting a boys' group pledge? Come on, the poor girl's probably starving to death. Look at her. A good stiff wind would blow her away. Why, she probably eats barely enough to keep body and soul together. I'm thinking we may have to take her under our wings, Nate. See to it she takes care of herself. Seems to me her family's falling down on the job.''

"Oh brother." Allie sighed softly. If he only knew. Allie was more than willing to let Ted do any repairs he wanted to attempt so long as they could keep her interfering family out of things. She'd be eighty and her father and brothers would dotter over on canes to smooth life's little wrinkles for her. She loved them all dearly, but sometimes she felt so...smothered.

Nate opened the car door for Allie, waited for her to climb in, then chuckled as he circled the vehicle. This was great. He'd forewarned her, so Allie couldn't say she hadn't known what to expect. Talk about taking lemons and making lemonade. He'd just bought himself a whole bunch of relative peace and quiet while his father was occupied at Allie's. Hot damn.

Oh sure, he knew what Ted was up to—and it wasn't only a repair job. Nate was wise to him now, thanks to overhearing his conversation with Allie earlier. But Nate wasn't worried about falling prey to any matchmaking. He was immune. But think about this. His father would be occupied for several days playing handyman and safely out of his hair. Unfortunately, it was going to cost Nate, at a time when his money should be plowed back into his new business, but the price would be well worth it. Heck, now that he thought about it, he was going to talk to Jared about deducting the repairs as a business expense. An extremely worthwhile business expense.

He drove to the hardware store, well aware of the disparaging glances Allie shot him from where she sat in the passenger seat. Well, good. He didn't want her to like him. He wasn't ready for anything permanent and this would keep things simple. He was grateful, yes, he was. If only she had a single mother, a maiden aunt he could recruit to keep Pop busy once the apartment repairs were taken care of, life would be perfect. He was on to his dad, but, heh-heh, he didn't think his dad was on to him.

Subtlety was lost on a man, Nate told himself as he drove, because men were usually so up-front about everything. But with a woman, a man had to be circumspect, come in the back door, otherwise women tended to get on their high horses and basically go ballistic. Well, no problem. Nate could lead a conversation, bring it around to where he wanted it to go without the other party even being aware. All he had to do was ask a few leading questions, get her talking. He'd find out everything there was to know about Allie and any unmarried female relatives without her being any the wiser.

"So, Allie," Nate started jovially, "tell us a little about yourself."

Lord, he wasn't *interested* in her, was he? Allie wondered. He was a good-looking guy and everything—really good-looking, to be honest, with his body by Apollo, wavy blond hair and Lake Michigan blue eyes. But she'd gotten vibes from Mr. Parker senior that Nate was having problems getting himself a woman who'd put up with him. And after conversing even briefly with the six-foot-plus Mr. Parker junior, Allie could understand why. Heck, the guy couldn't be loyal to his own father, talking him down the way he had. Her father made her crazy, too, but she didn't diss him. Not out loud. Not to a total stranger. She crossed her arms defensively over her chest. She wasn't interested. Absolutely not. And he didn't need to know anything about her. "Why do you want to know?"

Nate shrugged. "No reason. Just making conversation, that's all. You, um, come from a big family?"

"Not really."

Man, this was like pulling teeth. "Define not really."

"Brothers, okay? I've got three older brothers. They're great, but they all think I'm still ten. The three of them plus my father would be down here in nothing flat if they catch so much as a whiff of this. They'll have the repairs done—but to their specifications, not mine—and the entire place remodeled in a day and a half. They don't understand that I want to do things my way. Your dad at least asked my opinion on color and stuff. He's great," she finished, turning to smile at Ted in the back seat.

Nate shrugged. "Ceilings are white and carpet is supposed to be beige. For resale. A Realtor friend of mine told me that."

See? Just like her brothers. Allie rested her case.

Nate thought about her family description. Was there a problem with producing females in her family? Maybe this wasn't such a hot idea. Allie MacLord was cute in a Cathy Rigby with red hair gymnast kind of way. Nate assumed a female relative, provided she had some, would also be attractive. The problem, as he saw it, was cute really didn't stand up well against four large overprotective males who might misinterpret his interest in Allie. He'd go to the wall for the woman he'd eventually marry, of course, take on an entire legion if necessary, but that was years down the road. Years.

Nate tapped his fingers on the steering wheel while he thought about that. A trio of overgrown siblings on one side of the scale, his father on the other. Hmm. He could still be persuaded to take them on if the stakes were right. Like if an elderly maiden aunt could be found among her family members for his father. In fact, this was actually a no-brainer. If push came to shove, he'd take on the brothers and do it with a smile on his face. Nate made the decision to continue the interrogation, see if there was anything worth pursuing.

"How about your parents?" Were they conveniently divorced? Mom need a shoulder to cry on? Hey, it just so happened his dad had broad shoulders, for an older guy. When you thought about it, an interfering family and Allie's condo's proximity meant her relatives would be around a lot for his father to bump into. This could be good. Eagerly he awaited her response.

"There's just Dad," she reluctantly confided. Her large, gruff, love-you-till-he-smothers-you dad.

"Oh, really? Where's your mother?"

"She died. Breast cancer."

Oh, man. Nate winced and braked hard for a changing light, then turned to stare at her. "I'm sorry."

"It's okay. It was a while ago. I was sixteen."

Sixteen was a very vulnerable age. Damn.

Nate shot Allie a sideways look as he pulled into the parking lot for the hardware store, his gaze falling automatically to Allie's face. She still looked vulnerable. Like she was in need of protection. He had a sudden urge to pull over and wrap his arms around her. What, was he crazy? He ought to know better than to fall prey to his father's matchmaking.

"Nate, where are you planning on parking?" Ted wanted to know. "You've driven by three perfectly good spots. I know you're protective about your car, but do we really have to park at the far end of the lot?"

"What? Oh, sorry, Dad, I got distracted."

"I keep telling you, this isn't going to be that bad. We're both college graduates, aren't we? We can figure this out. Watch out for the light pole, will you?"

"Oops, sorry." He swerved, missed the pole in question and could feel a flush rising to stain his cheeks. Somehow that sudden spurt of feeling for Allie had gotten him positively flustered. *Damn it, get a grip, Parker,* he told himself. *You're acting like you're fifteen instead of thirty.* Like you've never seen breasts before.

Nate pulled into a spot and turned off the ignition. He leaned back in the seat for a moment to rein his thoughts in.

"Nate, you coming or what?"

"Yep. Right behind you two." And he was, he realized, after he got out of the car and locked it. He was also getting a great view of Allie's gently swaying derriere. She had a perky posterior Nate decided as he watched it swing through the turnstile in the front of the store. Decidedly perky.

"That all right with you, Nate?"

Nate's eyes rose guiltily from Allie's butt to the inquiring glance his father was sending back over his shoulder.

"Sure. What?"

Ted sighed. "Is it okay if, after we buy the guck and whatever tools we need to fix the ceiling, we go eat and then hit the mattress store? I'm starved and Allie just admitted she didn't have time for anything but an apple at lunchtime."

"No problem. We just have to be sure and replace Allie's mattress and bedding before the stores close."

Nate continued to watch Allie interact with his father as he trailed them around the store. She hadn't hesitated in showing *him* her vinegary side and yet she was being unfailingly polite and kind to his father. Allie smiled, made small talk and teased Ted. It was almost as though she sensed his father was needy and lonely and was doing her best to be kind.

Nate scowled at their backs. It wasn't like *he* hadn't figured out that much. He was every bit as damned perceptive. Nate just didn't know how to help his father, that was all. There was no need for him to feel like a worm, though, he

told himself. Think about it. Besides, his father was practically glowing in Allie's presence. If Nate played his cards
right, this whole situation could work to his advantage.
Pawning his dad off on Allie for a few days would buy
him some time to find a few older women to throw in Ted's
path, either from Allie's family or wherever. That would in
turn make his dad happy while keeping him occupied so
Nate could get a few things on his own accomplished.

He loved his father dearly.

He'd love him even more with a little distance worked
into their relationship.

Let's face it. He was being a heartless jerk dumping his
interfering father on an unsuspecting neighbor, but in a situation like this a little free time to concentrate on things
he needed to take care of in his professional and private
lives took precedence over fair play. No contest.

When they got to the appropriate section of the store,
there was a bit of a debate over what type of guck spreading
tools were appropriate. The store was busy, the help already
occupied. Nate ended up buying a couple of different ones,
picked at random. What did it matter? He was going to
have the whole thing redone in a couple of weeks anyway.
Let his dad play around however he wanted. He'd make it
up to Allie somehow. Nate shot Allie one of his best
woman-killer smiles.

She returned a look of suspicion and confusion.

Nate's eyes widened. Man, he must be losing his touch.
Guilt struck again. This really was a rotten thing to do to
someone. Now he knew how the high priests felt sacrificing
young virgins to the various vindictive gods. You didn't
have to like it, but a man's gotta do what a man's gotta
do. You just had to convince the virgin it was all for the
greater good. Nothing to it.

Was Allie MacLord still a virgin?

God, he hoped not. Because in the back of his mind Nate was entertaining some ideas about how he'd like to make it up to her once this mess was over and done with. It wouldn't be much of a hardship to, well, jump her bones. Nothing with strings attached or anything like that. No, just a mutual enjoyment kind of thing. Provided he could keep the overprotective males in her life and his father out of the picture, of course.

And he absolutely, positively would not feel guilty over letting his father try his hand at the repairs at Allie's place, even though it would double or triple the repair time. He'd warned her. All was fair in love and war, after all. Nor would he allow himself to feel badly for whatever female relative of Allie's he managed to lasso. Anyone could see his cause was just. Well, anyone but a woman. They loved being perverse. And half the time it was perversity for perversity's sake, which made it all the more frustrating.

Men, however, loved nothing better than a challenge. Nate figured he ought to be able to handle any roadblocks his father or a little bit like Allie could put in his way. They had met their match with Nathaniel Edward Parker. You bet they had.

Ignoring Allie's expression of confusion and his father's generally random choices from the stock in the drywall aisle, Nate shepherded his little flock of two to a checkout line. Ted made a production of paying, all the while still protesting his innocence. Nate let his dad pay without argument. It was too his fault.

It wasn't that much longer before Nate had everyone seated at a nearby restaurant. He rubbed his hands together. Life was good and Nate was starved. "So, what's everyone in the mood for?"

Allie gave him a glance and muttered, "Your head."

He was going to have to remember to bring earplugs—

or a gag—when it came time to jump her bones. "To eat, Allie. To eat."

Giving the menu a cursory glance, Allie announced, "Salad."

Nate looked at her doubtfully. "Salad? That's it? Just...salad?"

"Of course that's not it," his father interrupted. "What, does she look like a rabbit? The salad's just to start." Ted turned his attention to Allie, patted her hand. "Don't pay any attention to him, honey. Now what else do you want? Anything on the menu. Nate's paying. I bought the plastering stuff. Pick the most expensive thing they've got if that's what you want."

Nate rolled his eyes. "Dad, if she wants salad, she can have salad." He smiled apologetically at Allie.

"She doesn't want just salad. It's not healthy. She needs red meat. Look at her." Ted gestured with a hand. "Nothing to her. Chicken bones. Why a good breeze would blow her away. Pht" Ted made a flicking hand gesture. "There she goes."

"You don't know anything at all about women, do you, Pop?"

"What are you talking about? Of course I know women. I was married to one, wasn't I?"

"Yeah, and she always complained that you didn't understand her."

Ted snorted. "Your mother's mind was more convoluted than most and you know it." He aimed a finger at Nate. "Still, I had her pretty much figured out. Most of the time. I just didn't always agree with her and she'd feel like she had to complain a bit, that's all."

Nate looked at his father in amazement. His parents had been champion arguers. Champion. They'd also done a lot of kissing and making up, but still... He shook his head to clear it. "Whatever. The thing is, Dad, women read these female magazines, see, with these advice columns in them, okay? They think it's a turnoff if us guys see them eating a lot so they eat a bunch *before* they go out with a man so they're not that hungry. They don't want the guy to think they're not all delicate and feminine." Nate rubbed a hand over the top of his head. "I know you've seen *Gone with the Wind*. Mom used to watch it several times a year. The ladies loaded up before going to dinner so they wouldn't look like pigs in front of the men. What the ladies don't get, however, is that it ticks us off when we take them out to eat and they just pick at their food." He pointed a finger at Allie. "She probably snacked before we even got to her place."

"I did not!" Allie was incensed at the accusation. Like she cared what Mr. Nathaniel Parker thought. "I simply don't happen to be hungry tonight. Just because I don't eat like a truck driver is no reason—"

Ted patted her hand some more. "Now, now. Don't let him get you all upset. We'll just order you a hamburger. You look a little…what do you call it? Anemic, that's it. We gotta build your blood count up."

"Mr. Parker, it's okay. Really. I don't eat a lot of red meat. It's not good for you, you know."

"Ted, remember? We'll get you chicken, then. Look, here's a nice blackened chicken breast although I still say red—"

"I promise you there's nothing wrong with my blood count. I've got a lot of Irish in me. That's why I'm pale. Well, and I'm a little stressed at the moment, too, but it's mostly my heritage. See my freckles? Irish. And a little Scots."

Was he good or what? Nate thought.

"Are you folks ready to order?"

"Yes. I'd like the house salad, please. Light Italian dressing. Thank you."

"Chop some chicken on there for her, will you?" Ted directed. "She needs the protein. We're trying to build her up a little bit. Maybe some egg, too."

Allie gave up. "Fine. Put chicken on it. Put an egg on it. Use Geritol for the dressing. That ought to give me a blood count right off the charts and make everybody happy."

"Uh, I don't think we have any dressing like that."

Allie just sighed and put her head in her hands. "Mom, I really think you can do better than this. Honest to God, I really think you could. Put a little heart and soul into it, why don't you? Try harder, darn it."

Nate put a hand on Allie's shoulder, patted her soothingly. It was her first exposure to his father, after all. She was bound to be a bit stressed. "Excuse me? I didn't catch that. Can you lift your head? You're mumbling."

Allie turned her head out of her hands and glared at Nate. "I'm not talking to you."

"Oh, sorry. Dad, Allie's talking to you. Pay attention, will you?"

"Not him, either."

"Not him and not me. Fine. Then you were speaking to…whom?"

She glared harder. "If you must know, I was speaking to my mother. And it was a private conversation."

Nate cleared his throat. "Your mother? The one who's—"

"Yes, that's right. Frankly, I'm very disappointed in the way she's handling things up there and I just told her so. I'm sorry, but she could do a better job of watching out for me than she's currently doing. She *is* a lot nearer to the final seat of authority than I am, after all."

"Is that so?"

Allie nodded stubbornly. "Yes, that's so and that's just what I told her."

"Uh-huh. Okay, you told your mom off. Did she, um, have anything to say in return?" He held up his hands. "Just wondering."

"No, she doesn't talk back. Dead people don't, as a rule," Allie explained kindly. "Which doesn't mean she isn't listening, though," Allie stubbornly insisted. She raised her voice a little bit. "And I expect her to get her act together and do a better job."

"Oookay." Nate sat back in the booth, eyeing Allie warily. And she'd looked so normal. The waitress returned with their drinks. Nate took his and released the straw from its paper wrapper. He stuck it in his drink and sucked up half the liquid in his glass. So maybe he'd steer clear of Allie all together and forget even the mutually satisfying enjoyment of each other part of the deal. He might have been able to avoid the three brothers. Maybe even handle both fathers as well. But a knows-all, sees-all mother spirit? He didn't think so. And Nate liked his private life…private.

Chapter Three

Nate made it through dinner. He doubted he'd win the crown for Mr. Sociability, but he'd grunted a couple of times in response to direct questions and frankly, Nate doubted that either Allie or his father had much noticed his lack of participation. The two of them had managed a continual running conversation that Nate would have only interrupted had he tried to participate. So fine. To heck with them. Besides, wasn't this exactly what he'd been hoping for? It didn't hurt that his dad's attention had been so quickly and so thoroughly diverted. He might actually get a few constructive days in at work.

Allie and Ted continued to bond over brownie hot-fudge sundaes. An oddly disgruntled Nate picked up the tab. He held the restaurant door for Allie, who was so involved in her conversation with his father, she didn't even seem to notice the courtesy. Even so, Nate got the car door for her, closing it when she was safely seated. Darn, but for a short person she'd swung some long legs into the car.

Edgy for some reason, Nate paid extra attention to his driving as he made his way to the Sleep Factory.

"Of course I'm edgy," Nate muttered under his breath as he signaled a lane change. "I've had the day from perdition and by the time I'm finished just getting back to where I started from this morning, it'll probably have turned into the week from hell, possibly even the month from Hades."

"You say something, Nate?" his father asked.

"No."

"Humph." His father shrugged. "Thought you did. Oh, well, getting old. Allie, what about…"

Left out of the loop once more, Nate shook his head and pulled into the Sleep Factory's lot and parked.

Allie opened her door and swung her legs out. "Oh," she said when Nate showed up to offer her his hand since he couldn't open the door for her. "Oh. Thank you, Nate. I can manage on my own, but thank you."

"My mother taught me to treat a woman with respect."

Allie just looked at Nate, really seeing him for the first time. She'd been so involved in the mess her apartment had become, she hadn't really *processed* what had been right there in front of her. Hard to believe. Nate was tall, over six feet, she'd bet. From her seated position, he towered over her. She'd thought him blond, but now that she was noticing, it was really all streaky with different shades of blond and light brown all mixed together as though he spent a lot of time in the sun—or paid a lot to a hairdresser. Somehow she doubted Nate Parker spent a lot of time in a beauty parlor. His eyes were blue. There was the beginning of crinkles around their corners and his skin was lightly tanned. He reminded her a lot of this lifeguard she'd had a crush on when she'd been sixteen. She'd never gotten him to notice her that whole summer. If it hadn't been for the plumbing going berserk in Nate's apartment, she doubted she'd be spending time with him, either. Allie tried to be honest, especially with herself. She just wasn't the type to inspire lust in modern-day Apollos. Maybe her mother had burst his pipe for him? No, that was too ridiculous.

"Well?" Nate asked, his hand still stuck out there. "You coming or what?"

Allie swallowed. Yes, yes she was. Allie gave Nate her hand and let him draw her up and out of the car. "Thank you," she said.

Nate looked at her oddly. "You're welcome." He closed the door, locked it and then put his hand on the small of Allie's back to guide her into the store.

She shivered.

"Cold?" he asked.

"No, I'm okay." She wasn't but she wasn't really sure how to explain what was wrong with her and wasn't about to try, not to Nate. A guy who looked like him probably already had a swelled head; no way was Allie going to add to it. A second shiver went down her spine.

"Sure?"

"Yes, really."

They entered the store, both the men standing back, allowing her to be first. Allie glanced around.

"Oh, Lord," she murmured. She'd been so thrilled that her unknown neighbor hadn't given her a hard time about replacing her mattress, she hadn't considered the shopping-for-it-with-him aspect. Allie stood just inside the door, staring at an entire showroom of mattresses. Mattresses she should lie on to check for comfort before purchasing. Lie down on in front of Nate Parker. "Oh, Lord. Mom?" She whispered, rolling her eyes heavenward.

"Hey, can we come in, too?"

Allie turned. Nate and Ted were bottlenecked in the en-

tryway behind her. Allie stepped to the side. "Sorry,"
she said.

Ted stepped confidently forward, rubbing his hands together. "All right, boys and girls. Look at this, will you?
Mattress heaven right here on earth. We'll find you a replacement bed in nothing flat, Allie girl, wait and see."

Allie certainly hoped so. She'd never gone bed shopping
with a handsome eligible bachelor before. It was suddenly
all a little too intimate for her, sort of like underwear shopping with her brothers before she'd gotten her license and
they'd had to chauffeur her around, only worse, much
worse. Ted was *not* her father and Nate was *not even close*
to being her brother. Allie did not want to drag the task
out any longer than absolutely necessary.

Taking a deep breath, Allie bravely stepped forward. She
took exactly six steps to the closest display. "How about
this one right here?" she asked, more than willing to take
the sample, if need be and run with it.

Ted quickly put the kibosh on that brilliant scheme.
"You can't just buy it without trying it out, sweetie. Come
on, have a lie down." Ted patted the mattress invitingly.

"Oh, no, really. I'm sure it's fine."

Ted made a dismissing gesture. "It's kind of skinny
compared to the one over there, don't you think? Let's take
a look around. I'm betting we can find one you'll like even
better."

"Dad, she said this one would be fine." The price on
the one his father was pointing to was twice the cost of
Allie's first choice.

Ted was not to be stopped or even stalled. "It's like
shopping for a Christmas tree. You think you've found a
good one until you look in the next row over. There's always a better one." He waggled a finger at Nate and Allie.

"A better one you'll never find if you don't look beyond the first one you see."

Nate rubbed his temples where a headache was beginning to develop. "Just do it, Allie. Get it over with or you'll never hear the end of it. Trust me on this." Putting his two hands at her waist, Nate picked Allie up and gently dropped her on the mattress. "Lie down," he said.

"But…"

Gently Nate put a hand on her forehead and pushed her flat. "What do you think?" he asked.

She thought insanity probably ran in the Parker family line, that's what she thought. "Uh, good. It's good."

Nate nodded, picked her up and carried her to the next display where he carefully dropped her. "And this one?"

As Nate carried Allie from one bed to the next, Allie had trouble concentrating. Who wouldn't? "You'll hurt your back!" she'd said, worried at first.

"Please," Nate had disputed while rolling his eyes. "Let's not get insulting. You're such a lightweight I'm surprised there's enough of you for gravity to get a good grip on."

"Trust me, there's enough." But Nate certainly didn't seem to be breathing hard, turning red in the face or straining as he carted her from bed to bed. Not only was Nate a hunk, a hunk of burning love, he was one *strong* hunk of burning love. Finally they honed in on a choice that made Ted and Allie both happy.

"Now," Ted said, still smiling even though they'd circled around the store only to end up back with Allie's first pick. "We just have to decide on the size."

Allie looked up in surprise. "What? Well, twin, of course. I mean, that's what we're replacing, after all."

"Ah." Ted made a dismissing gesture. "Twin, shwin. Barely enough room for you in there. Come on, live a little,

Allie girl. Plan ahead. You may not be sleeping with any-body now, but a good mattress should last fifteen, twenty years, hmm? What if you meet the man of your dreams in the next year or two? You gonna just toss out a mattress with all kinda life left in it and start over?'' Ted shook his finger at her. ''That's not practical, now, is it? What if you meet Mr. Wonderful next month? Next week?'' Ted raised his brows and leaned in. ''What if you met him today?'' he tilted his head meaningfully toward Nate and nodded at her.

''All right, Dad, that's enough,'' Nate got out between clenched teeth.

''What?'' his father protested innocently. ''What'd I do? All I said was…''

''We heard what you said, Dad. Now, behave. You're making Allie uncomfortable.'' To say nothing of the fact Nate himself was starting to sweat. He wasn't too sure if it was irritation with Ted over the way he was trying to manipulate the situation or the mental imagery of Allie sharing a bed with some guy, say, oh, one Nathaniel E. Parker, for example.

Ted put an arm around each of their shoulders in seeming companionability. ''Seriously now, kids. The sample here's a queen size. Both of you have a lie down, now.''

Allie and Nate leaned slightly forward so they could see each other's faces around Ted's bulk.

Things were becoming a bit too surrealistic for Nate. ''Dad…''

''Mr. Parker…''

''Ted,'' he immediately corrected. ''Come on. It's per-fectly innocent. We're in the middle of a store, for crying out loud. And I promise, I have no ulterior motives. Really. Now, Nate, just lie there for a minute so Allie can decide between queen- and king-size.''

Nate rolled his eyes. He loved his father dearly, but it was going to be a close call as to whether or not that filial devotion kept the old man physically safe from his ever-loving son because dear old Dad, regardless of his protestations of innocence had said what he'd said purposely. And the purpose? To make Nate start thinking about Allie in bed…with Nate.

And what aggravated Nate the most?

It was working.

Oh, yeah. Theodore Parker was one devious man. Nate would have been far more admiring if that deviousness had been directed some other way, however. If Nate couldn't find him a wife, maybe the CIA would be interested. It was a thought.

Nate plopped down on the bed and practically threw himself backward. He crossed his arms belligerently over his chest and glared up at his father. "There. I'm down. Happy now?"

Ted shook his head. "Never mind him, Allie, honey. Just lie down and see how it feels. There you go. Is it still comfortable? You're not going to roll into him, are you? My wife and I had a bed once that sank in the middle. If you didn't hang on to the edge for dear life, we'd roll and end up practically on top of each other in the center."

His father was killing him here. Killing him. All Nate could think about was being in the middle of a bed with Allie and, frankly, he didn't much care which one of them ended up on top.

"You wouldn't want a bed like that," Ted continued.

Says who? Nate thought.

"Remember how this one feels."

It would be a while before Nate forgot. Oh, wait. His father was talking to Allie, not him.

"And let's go over and try the king. Are you hot-blooded or cold-blooded, Allie?"

His dad just wouldn't quit, would he? Honest to God, you almost had to admire the way he came out with one zinger after another. Until this moment in time, Nate wouldn't have believed him capable of it. Nate's whole body was going hot just thinking about the answer to this one. She was hot-blooded. Some women, you could tell by looking, and Allie had too much passion for it to not carry over into bed. He knew it.

Allie looked a little taken aback by the question, however. "Excuse me?" she said.

"It might make a difference in your choice, is all," Ted justified, the picture of innocence.

Yeah, right. But Nate was determined to keep his mouth shut. Every time he opened it, Ted stuck his foot in it anyway.

Ted patted the king-size mattress they'd approached. "On a bed like this, there'll be more room. You won't be as close, if there are two of you in it." Ted made a gesture and Allie obediently reclined. "See, if you're hot-blooded, you might want your spouse way over there. Otherwise, you might overheat or something."

Oh, good Lord.

"On the other hand, if you get cold easy, why, the queen-size would be perfect. Snuggle right up to him, take advantage of all that shared body heat, you know?"

Ted cleared his throat and looked as if he was pondering the secrets of the universe. "As nearly as I can tell, this all boils down to one simple question."

Like his father had ever let anything remain simple in his whole life.

"Are you or are you not a snuggler?"

"A snuggler?" Allie felt her face starting to heat. She

jumped out of the bed as though the mattress had caught fire. Allie noticed Nate also rose, though more slowly. Evidently he was far more comfortable with this type of discussion than she was. The day had really been strange and the evening was doing its best to keep pace. She was not used to intimate discussions taking place with virtual strangers. She could hardly tell him it was none of his business, however. The man was trying to help her pick out a bed he was going to pay for, after all. She supposed it was a logical question and maybe it would be silly to purchase another twin. Allie had every intention of marrying someday. She wanted children. She just wanted to experience a little personal freedom first. Then she hoped to find some guy who'd appreciate what a gem she was. But that was for the future. Not here, not now. Which was a good thing because it didn't take a Mensa member to figure out the guy next to her was not *the one*. Nate Parker was impatient, his manners only begrudgingly displayed, and he seemed chronically irritated with everyone, even his own father.

"Once again, Dad, how's she supposed to know if she's a cuddler?"

And Allie was getting darn tired of Nathaniel Parker acting like she'd just hatched from an egg and was some kind of naive young pullet. "I've had boyfriends," she burst out, thoroughly irritated with his know-it-all attitude. "Plenty of them." Now she sounded as though she was bragging. Great. Would this evening never end?

"But have any of them qualified as a significant other?" Nate waggled his eyebrows meaningfully.

Allie frowned at him. "None of your business."

"See? I knew it. They weren't," Nate insisted.

"See what? How would you know?"

"I can tell."

"Oh, really. How?" Allie's hands were on her hips and she was definitely crowding Nate's personal space.

You had to give the woman credit, Nate thought, although he still didn't believe she'd had much experience. She was right in his face, doing her best to intimidate him. He almost snorted, as if that would work. "I just can."

"Children, children," Ted chided, "this is counterproductive. Let's not waste our time arguing. We'll settle this here and now. Nate, come up behind Allie and put your arms around her. Snuggle up to her back. We'll see if she likes it or not."

"What!" Allie exclaimed.

"For the love of…" Nate swore under his breath. If he'd just kept his mouth shut the way he'd intended, but no, he'd had to open his big yap. What had he been thinking? He hadn't, that was the problem. Yes he had. The mental image of Allie spooning up with some guy in a bed Nate had bought her, well, it didn't sit well, that was all. So what had Nate done? Played right into his father's hand, that's what. Nate had known darn well Ted's main goal here was to drive him crazy. Replacing Allie's mattress was only the current tool he was using.

"You are going to burn in hell," he informed his father. "Come here, Allie. Let's get this over with." He just hoped her mother's back was turned away up there in the netherworld. He didn't need his backside zapped should she take offense.

"But…"

"Nathaniel, you wound me."

He wasn't buying it. "Yeah, right. Whatever." As a matter of fact, Nate resolved then and there that he was going to find a woman who would drive his father crazy for the rest of his natural life. If he had to sell out to Jared and devote himself full-time to the project, that's what he'd do.

Whatever it took. "Allie, come on. Let's get this over with."

"But…"

"You don't honestly think we're going to get away without doing it?" Of course they could. All they had to do was ignore his father, which would hurt his feelings, call the salesman over, pay for the thing and leave. Heck, they could leave now and come back later to purchase the mattress just the two of them. But even though he knew giving in to his father would only encourage his antics, Nate's arms itched to see how Allie would fit in them. Reaching out, Nate put a hand on Allie's shoulder, gently twirling her about so her back was to him. "Let's just humor him."

"Nate…" Allie began nervously.

"Shh." Eyeballing Allie, he realized he'd be able to tuck her right under his chin. Nate took a step forward, then guided her back to the bed, his chest bumping into her back. Lying back down, Nate slid his arms around her waist, roping her in closer. Yep, he'd been right, she could have been custom-ordered for him. His shoulders curved around her back, his chin rested on the top of her head, a few strands of baby-fine hair snagged in his five-o'clock shadow. Allie's hair was soft and tickled. It smelled like some kind of flower. "So." Nate had to pause and clear his throat. "What do you think?"

She thought about the fact that it was the middle of September and winter was on its way. That fall nights had already cooled way down. And that if she could keep Nate Parker at her back, she'd never be cold again. She thought that if Nate would come home with her, she could kiss her flannel pajamas goodbye and donate her wool socks to Goodwill, that's what she thought. Allie felt really, really…warm. She sighed with pleasure.

His dad actually snorted, he was so pleased with himself,

the old coot. "I think she likes it, Nate," he contributed, although nobody'd asked him for his opinion, certainly not Nate or Allie. "So, what do you think, Allie? Queen?"

Allie wiggled back against Nate, seeking out more of that wonderful, furnacelike source of heat before she realized what she was doing. She immediately turned red and tried to wiggle away.

Nate refused to release her. He figured she might have felt, uh, something inappropriate pressing again her back and was embarrassed. He probably should be as well, but she just felt too good in his arms to let go just yet. Nate guessed this wasn't very gentlemanly of him and he was sorry for that, but he was only human. Nate thought he'd developed far more control as he'd gotten older, but...*wrong.* And if she'd just think about it, it was actually a compliment. Still, it seemed to be making her uncomfortable. Considering Allie's obvious lack of experience, Nate supposed that was totally understandable, more was the pity. She sure felt good there in his arms. Nate sighed regretfully and grudgingly gave her a bit more leeway. His arms were enjoying themselves a little too much for Nate to let go of Allie entirely, however. And she might as well know up-front that if she wanted to sleep spooned up to a guy she was going to encounter some things she might not have encountered yet. All in all, Nate decided to think of it as a public service coming under the heading Things You Ought To Know or some such thing. "Allie?"

"Queen," Allie said, her voice sounding breathy to her own ears. Oh, yeah. Definitely queen.

Ted scratched his chin. "Probably a good choice," he said. "Give you more floor space in your bedroom and the sheets and stuff are no doubt cheaper. Less material and all that."

Oh, yeah. His dad had been thinking of the practicalities

when he'd suggested they torture each other by embracing on the bed. Sure. Irritation with his father's generally sneaky ways finally got Nate to let go and sit back up. "You sure, honey?" Oops, he hadn't meant to say that.

He'd called her honey. Allie swallowed hard. "It felt nice," she said lamely, her posture stiff as she sat up herself. "All except for the belt. Your buckle was up against my back, but a man wouldn't wear a belt to bed. And you're right. You sure generate a lot of heat. If all men are like you and I find the right one for me, I could kiss cold toes goodbye for the rest of my life. It felt warm and…just nice, I guess," Allie finished. She was trying to be nonchalant about this whole thing, but it was darn difficult. She didn't usually go mattress-shopping with men she barely knew.

Nate froze, his eyes wide. Was she for real? Allie thought he'd been poking her with his *belt buckle?* But she'd assured him she wasn't naive, that she'd had boyfriends, significant others even.

Right.

Allie MacLord was a virgin and that was that.

Chapter Four

Sensing some kind of consensus had been reached by the threesome the way only a clerk on commission could do, the salesman closed in. "Help you folks?"

Ted answered before Nate or Allie could get their mouths open. "Yes. We want one of these. Queen-size."

"Very nice choice. One of our bestsellers. In fact…"

"You don't need to sell us. We're already talked into it and we're kind of in a hurry seeing as how it's getting late and we still have to get it all set up. Could you just write up the ticket?"

"Please," Allie threw in, evidently afraid of offending the salesman.

Nate rolled his eyes. The guy was going to get a hefty commission. He doubted his father's lack of a "please" was going to make him walk away in a huff. "Yeah, Dad," he said just for the fun of heckling. "Don't forget your manners. Pleases are gold and thank-yous are silver, remember."

"Huh?"

"I'm happy to help you," the salesman hastily intervened, evidently not wanting a family argument to break out before he got hold of somebody's credit card. "And we can do this relatively quickly, but I'm afraid you won't be able to take it with you."

"What?"

"What?"

"Why not?"

The salesman took a step back. "I would if I could," he hastily assured the group. "But this is just the showroom. The mattresses come from the warehouse. I can have it delivered by the day after tomorrow."

"Not good enough," Ted growled.

"Where is the warehouse? Can we go pick it up?" queried Allie.

"You'd never get there before nine," the salesman assured them. "And it will take them a while to pull it from stock."

"Well." Allie sighed philosophically. "I guess it's the floor for me."

"You're not sleeping on the floor," Nate said, dismissing the idea out of hand. "I doubt the carpet's had time to dry out anyway." There was a hotel not too far away, he thought. He guessed he'd be springing for a night.

"That's all right. Nate's got plenty of room at his place. You'll stay there. He's got a nice long sofa you can camp on till we get you a replacement. In fact—" his father turned on him "—Nate, you can take the sofa and give little Allie here your bed. She's the guest, after all."

"Dad!"

"What? It's just basic good manners."

"I only have two love seats in my living room and they're too short. I should have gotten a sofa instead," Allie fretted.

"Too late to worry about should-have-dones now," Ted imparted philosophically.

"True. Very true. But still, I can't sleep in...not in Nate's *bed*."

"I don't have cooties," Nate snapped, thoroughly disgruntled with both his father for offering and Allie for acting so horrified by the idea. A lot of women would be more than happy to have a spot in his bed. Why, he could probably sell tickets. If he wanted. He was very discerning, that was all. Besides, if Allie was in such close communication with her mother, it made him sort of wonder where his own mom was when Nate chose to...entertain. It wasn't a particularly edifying mental picture, that was for sure.

Cooties were not what Allie had been worried about. "I never thought you did," Allie said. "It's just that I don't want to put you out." That, and she was beginning to suspect she might have a bit of a heart problem. The little time she'd spent mattress testing with Nate definitely had her little heart going pitter-patter. Sleeping in his bed even without him in it with her might just send the poor thing smack into defibrillation. The sheets would be permeated with his heady masculine scent even if they were freshly laundered, she just knew it. Allie would smell him all night long. The pillow beneath her head would be one she'd know usually cradled his head with its thick blond hair. Just the mental image had her pulse rate jumping. "And I don't sleep well in a strange bed." Especially not his, Allie suspected.

Ted turned to the salesman. "Her bed was ruined through no fault of her own. My son's sink sprang a leak and flooded out the place beneath his. That's how they met. Isn't there something you can do?"

"I'm really sorry." He made a helpless, fluttering gesture with his hands. "But there's nothing, at least not tonight. The best would be to put a rush on it and have the mattress there sometime tomorrow.''

Allie sighed and rubbed her nose in a gesture of frustration. ''If that's the best you can do, then that's the best you can do.''

The salesman guided them over to the cash register station and got all the pertinent information. Allie insisted on paying the difference between the twin and queen size. She took the receipt.

''Just until it's delivered,'' she told Nate. ''Then you can have it to give the insurance company. Tell them how much of it you paid. Maybe they'll reimburse part. Oh, and hang on to the hardware receipt, too. You can probably claim that as well. How much is your deductible?''

''Uh, you know, I'm not sure.'' He wasn't about to tell her, make her feel bad.

''Well, maybe, if it's not too high, you won't be out too much.''

Even if the deductible wasn't high, which it was, Nate would still be out his peace of mind. Now that he knew what was one floor down, Nate expected a lot of sleepless nights. He had an excellent imagination, one that had a mind of its own. Especially when he emptied it of a day's worth of extraneous clutter—like when he was trying to sleep. Visions of Allie were bound to dance through his head. Allie, especially sans clothing would be as sweet as any sugar plum fairy could hope to be. Nate ran a hand over his head. Damn, what with trying to stay on top of his business and keep up with his father, he needed his sleep.

''I'm sure I'll be fine, regardless of the deductible,'' Nate told her. ''Don't worry about me. Let's just get you back in business.''

Delivery arrangements were made for the next day. Nate,

Ted and Allie left. The salesman locked up behind them. It was a few minutes after nine.

"Next step, home," Allie murmured as she slid into the car's front seat. She put her head back and closed her eyes. Her fingers pinched the bridge of her nose then touched her temples.

"Headache?" Nate inquired.

"I'm thinking about one," Allie admitted. "I'm going to fix myself a cup of tea first thing when we get back. Maybe I can stave it off."

Ted leaned forward in the back seat, rested his elbows on the back of the seat in front of him. "You've had a rough day," he said. "Go on up to Nate's place when we get back. Let him make the tea for you." Ted shot Nate a look, daring him to object, then promptly removed himself from the equation. "My car's in front of your building. When we get there, I'll just keep on going. Old guy like me, I need my sleep. You can handle a cup of tea by yourself, right, Nate?"

Enough was enough. His father had all the subtlety of a sledgehammer being used to tap in a tack. "Yes, I can make tea, Dad. I'll have to borrow it from Allie since I don't drink it, especially not the herbal stuff and I doubt she wants any caffeine this late at night, but I believe I can handle it. Tell me this, though. Did it ever occur to you that it might be us that's giving her the headache? Maybe Allie just wants to be alone for a while."

Ted immediately denied the possibility his company could be anything but exhilarating. "Don't be ridiculous."

God, he was thick.

"It's everything that's happened," his father insisted. "Anyone would have a headache."

"I've had the same rotten day," Nate pointed out. "Worse since I'm stuck with cleaning up both places as well as the bills for everything. And I don't have a head-ache.''

Ted snorted. ''That's because your head is full of rocks. You've got to be more sensitive to other people, Nate. That's what women want, I hear. A man who's in touch with his feminine side.''

He'd rather eat dirt. ''It would be a whole lot easier if women got in touch with their masculine side, don't you think? But they never think of that. They're too busy trying to *change* us. Maybe we don't *want* to be changed.''

''You guys plan to spend a lot of time by yourselves, I guess.'' Allie said, unable to resist the gibe.

''Never mind him.'' Ted dismissed Nate with a wave of his hand. ''Where do you work, Allie? Can you sleep in tomorrow?''

''No,'' Allie responded regretfully. ''I can't sleep in. I'm a school teacher. I have to get up early. It takes a while to get there.''

''Where?'' Nate asked.

''St. Stephen the Martyr. It's in Englewood. You know how bad traffic on the Kennedy and Ryan is. Then 59th has a light on just about every corner.''

''Englewood! That's one of the worst areas of Chicago!'' Nate exclaimed.

''I know,'' Allie said.

''Does your family…''

''Yes, they know and are very unhappy over it. Trust me, they've made their displeasure clear.''

A lightbulb had just gone off in his head. ''You know, Dad, Allie teaches in the inner city. She's used to stress and rough days. She's made of tough stuff.''

Allie's brows rose. ''Why, thank you.''

''You're welcome. Still, working in the inner city's hard,

I imagine. You probably do get a lot of headaches and stuff.''

"Some," Allie allowed. She reached behind her and patted the arm Ted had resting on her seat back. ''But there's no need for either one of you to fuss," she assured them both. "I can zap a cup of water in the microwave for tea and no doubt be fine. If not, some painkillers will do the trick.''

Nate ruthlessly cut in before his father could even get started. If he wasn't careful his father would have Allie moved right into his apartment and into his bed. Hell, he'd have them *married* before you could blink. When and if he ever decided to marry, and that was a big if, Nate was going to darn well pick his own bride, thank you very much. On the other hand, however opposed he was to the matrimonial state for himself, Nate had no qualms about shackling his father in one place. His mother had been gone for two incredibly long years, at least by Nate's estimation, now. If marriage was the key to happiness, how come his old man wasn't remarried? Why was that?

"You heard her, Dad," Nate said, determined to divert his father's attention. "Allie gets these headaches all the time. Probably stress. Tension, too. And who can blame her?" he asked generously. "Inner city schools, bound to be chock-full of stress and tension. Guns, knives, who knows what all. Whole staff probably has tension headaches.''

Ted's eyes narrowed as he considered that. "Saints, every one of them," he declared, canonizing the whole group with one sweeping statement. "Allie, what was your father thinking, letting you go into that neighborhood everyday? Why your mother's probably rolling over in her grave right now. Nate, you're going to have to check this place out....''

"Can't, Dad. I work, remember?"

"Yes, but—"

"You, on the other hand, took early retirement."

"Yes, but—"

God, it felt good to be the one cutting his father off, for a change. It was time to turn the tables on him. Heck, it was time and then some. "You could go in there, keep an eye on things. Do some reading on school security, check the locks out. Keep those living saints alive, you know?"

Allie finally managed to get a word in edgewise. "The school's not like that. It's parochial. There are no weapons of any type. The kids can't even bring a nail clipper in. The parents work two and three jobs because they don't want their children in the public schools where it's much more dangerous. It's very secure. Believe me, my dad and brothers already checked it out. The building is kept locked down while school is in session. School starts an hour earlier than the public schools and gets out that much sooner as well, so our kids don't get hassled coming or going. I'm perfectly safe."

Nate rubbed his chin, steered with one hand, as he considered that. There had to be some way to get his father involved. "So these are the kids whose parents really, really want them to succeed?"

"Yes."

"How are their standardized test scores?"

"They do all right," Allie said. "Way better than the public schools. The scores are just not as high as they could be."

"What do they need to get them up there? In your opinion." Nate paralleled into a spot just behind his father's car.

"How much time do you have?"

"What I'm hearing is that you could use some volunteers

at your place. I mean, a lower adult to student ratio would mean better learning, right?''

Ted leaned farther over the seat. "What're you thinking, son?''

Nate shrugged. "I don't know, Dad. My background is business and finance, not education. Allie here's the expert. But, from what she's said, I bet her school would love someone to come in and read stories to the kids, tutor them a bit in math or English, maybe be an aide in a classroom now and again to help maintain order so more teaching could take place.''

"An art and a music teacher would be wonderful along with some classroom aides,'' Allie admitted.

"Don't look at me. I can't sing.''

"Yes, you can,'' Ted immediately contradicted. "You were picked for Voices Across America in both your sixth and seventh grades.''

Nate was impressed his father knew that. Nate hadn't realized he'd been paying attention back then. He snorted anyway. "They'd have taken any boy that was warm and breathing. I was the only guy willing to open my mouth. Singing was not cool in the sixth and seventh grade.'' Damn, he was getting sidetracked again. How did his father do it? "And I'm not the one with the free time, Dad. You are.''

His father opened the car door, got out and stretched. Nate and Allie climbed out as well. Nate was not going to let this drop. There had to be some unmarried older ladies at Allie's place. The spinster schoolteacher had to have become a stereotype for a reason, didn't it? Even if Ted didn't meet the spinster lady of his dreams, he'd be occupied and out of Nate's hair. Best of all? Nate didn't even need to feel guilty about his machinations. Ted would be busy performing good deeds in Nate's name. A real win-win sort of deal. It was too perfect.

His father finished his stretch. "Come on, Nate. What good would an old man like me be? They need somebody young and strong."

"You weren't listening, Dad. Allie doesn't need a pro-tector. She needs somebody to come in and read stories to one group while she works with another. Somebody to help the slower ones with math problems." Nate made a hand gesture toward his father. "You'd be perfect. You used to read me stories."

"Not enough."

"Well, I'm too old to read to now. Do it where it will do some good. Come on."

Ted scratched his head. "I don't know. Don't they have stuff like new math now?"

"Two and two are still four, Dad."

"I'll think about it."

He'd do more than think about it, but Nate thought he'd probably pressed enough for now. "Sure, Dad, you think about it. Go on home and get some sleep. I'm going to take Allie in and get her settled."

His father was evidently eager to leave the two of them alone together. Maybe he was hoping propinquity would propink. Fat chance. Ted had been so blatant, Nate had been onto him almost from the get-go. His guard was well and truly up. Still Ted immediately agreed. "Right. You two go on up. Allie's got to be dead on her feet. Take care of her, Nate. I'll just be getting along. Don't want to miss the news."

Nate rolled his eyes but refrained from saying anything. His dad was working on his own agenda, but then again, so was Nate. May the better man win.

"Night, Ted."

"Night, honey. I'll be in touch. I'll be over to take care of things soon as it's all had a chance to dry out. Probably take a few days then Nate and I will have everything back right as rain before you know it."

She could only hope. "That would be great. See you whenever."

Ted smiled, wavered for a moment, then pulled Allie in for a hug. Nate rolled his eyes once more and tugged Allie away from his father. He kept a hand on her arm as he separated the two, then guided Allie to the apartment door. "Later, Dad."

"Yeah. Take care of Allie, you hear?"

"Uh-huh. No prob." The door swished shut, effectively cutting off any more conversation. Nate breathed a sigh of relief. He walked with Allie up the stairs to the second floor. "I apologize for my father, Allie. Taking an early retirement was a mistake for him. Too much time on his hands has made him a meddler. That and I think he's still missing Mom."

Allie felt a tug of sympathy. "It took my dad a while to get over Mom's death. How long has it been?"

"Two years."

"Oh." After all that time together, it was probably tough to go it solo. Her own father kept very busy. It was his way of coping. Maybe Nate's idea for his father to do volunteer work wasn't such a bad one. "Has he gotten any help? You know, from a professional?"

"You mean like a shrink?"

"Well, yeah."

"Fat chance. His generation would need to develop fifteen extra personalities before they'd admit to head problems."

"How about you?"

"Me?" Nate held the stairwell door for Allie, and let her precede him into the second-floor hallway.

"Yes, you. Maybe if *you* talked to someone…"

Nate was heartily insulted. "There's nothing wrong with my head. Dad's the one with the problem. I have a life, or at least I would if I could get my dad to ease up a little. *I* certainly don't need to talk to anyone."

Okay, that was the wrong tack to take. Evidently it wasn't just the older generation who had a problem admitting they needed help coping. "Hey, it doesn't make you a candidate for an insane asylum. I've gone and talked to people a few times myself when I was going through a difficult patch."

Why was he not surprised? She probably required it on a regular basis. For sure she left a wake of people behind her who needed it.

"It was very helpful."

Yeah, well she'd probably be back for another helping of psychobabble stew once she'd been around his father for a while. "It's all right for you. You're a girl."

"Oh, please."

"Seriously."

Allie just shook her head. What a Neanderthal. She stuck her key in her apartment door.

Nate's head swung up along as the door opening widened. "What's that smell?" he wanted to know. He hadn't noticed any pets when he'd been in her apartment earlier. "Smells like something died."

Allie's nose wrinkled up. "It does smell bad, doesn't it? And why was the door so hard to open? And why is it so warm in here?"

They entered the apartment together. Nate noticed the clock on the stove was blinking. "The power must have been out while we were away."

"That means the floor fans we set up weren't working the whole time we were gone. I don't know about your place, but this one heats up really fast when the air-conditioning's not on. We left all the windows shut when we left because central air dehumidifies." Allie covered her mouth and nose with a hand. "It's really sour smelling in here. Yuck!"

Nate had turned back to close the front door. It was a struggle. "Your door's all swollen from the moisture in here," he told her. "Now that we got it open, I don't think we'll get it shut again to lock it."

"That's great. Just great," Allie announced as she raised her arms, then let them drop in a gesture of defeat. Ted was a nice old guy and it was obvious that he was lonely. Not surprising, with a son who seemed to begrudge giving him the time of day. He'd been so eager to please, but he hadn't really listened to her. Understandable. The guy hadn't had any daughters. Rather than put up a fuss, Allie had been just waiting for him to go home. She'd really intended to camp out in her living room. Maybe pull the cushions off the love seat, throw them on the floor to sleep on so she'd be more comfortable. "It's really awful in here, isn't it?"

It was pretty darn bad, he'd give her that. Nate really wanted to hit something. Man, could anything else go wrong today? He was almost afraid to go upstairs and check his messages. The company had probably gone under in the few hours he'd been out of contact. That was about the only thing left that could happen. He took a deep breath and held it while he silently counted to ten. He sighed. "Dad's right. You can't stay here tonight. I'll help you gather up whatever you think you'll need. You'll have to stay with me, I guess."

Well, how very gracious of him. He guessed she'd have

to stay with him? Allie didn't think so. "That's okay. I'll figure something out. Maybe if I open a window and—"

"Allie, you can't even lock your front door!" Nate exploded. "You wouldn't be safe!"

"All right, all right. Watch your blood pressure there, Nate. I can, um, go to a hotel. There. That's safe. I'll just go stay at a hotel. No problem."

"Allie, please. Just let me help you get what you need and come upstairs with me. Dad finds out you stayed at a hotel, I'll never hear the end of it."

"But—"

"Please, I'm begging you. No more arguing. Just do it, okay? I'm developing a headache myself. It feels strong enough to fry every circuit in my brain and after my teenage rebellious beer-swilling period, I can't afford to lose any more brain cells."

Thoughtfully, Allie chewed her lower lip while she considered her options. If her father ever found out she'd stayed in an apartment with some man she barely knew, he'd have heart failure and be all over her case. On the other hand, her front door *wouldn't* lock, it stunk to high heaven in here and she really couldn't afford a hotel. Not on her pay. She'd be perfectly justified asking Nate to pay for one, but she didn't want to impose any more financial burdens on him. What to do?

Allie shrugged. Sometimes you just went with your gut. "Okay," she said. She'd bring her cell phone with her. Sleep with it under her pillow. Nine-one-one was programmed into her speed dial. She'd also make a point of letting a neighbor know where she was and with whom. That should do it. Nodding to herself, Allie put words into action. "I don't need that much stuff—my toothbrush, nightgown, nothing I can't carry on my own. And I need to stop next door and let Mrs. Klegman know where I'll be. She's, uh, got health problems—'' which would be news to the elderly but vibrant widow ''—and I told her she should call me anytime if she needed help. Go on up. I'll be there shortly.''

''You sure?''

Allie nodded.

''Well, okay.''

''Well,'' said Allie as she took in Nate's retreating back. ''Maybe my virtue's perfectly safe after all. No worries. He couldn't get out of here fast enough. Huh.'' Allie considered that. She wasn't sure if she should be happy to have her fears put to rest or insulted that she could evidently rest easy. Men. Who could figure them?

Allie went through the apartment, gathering up what she'd need. Her toothbrush and nightgown. Moisturizer and makeup. A hairbrush. Clean underwear, socks and a shirt for morning. A book to read till she fell asleep. Her own pillow. She tucked all that plus a few other essentials into the pillowcase and rang Mrs. Klegman's doorbell. Better to be safe than sorry.

But would she? Be sorry, that was.

''Well, of course I would be,'' she said out loud, horrified by the direction of her thought. ''Of course I would be sorry. Good grief.'' Allie leaned harder on the bell. Finally the door opened as far as a safety chain would allow it. ''Who is it?''

Allie slanted her head so Mrs. Klegman could see her face through the crack of the opening. ''It's me, Mrs. Klegman. Allie.''

''Allie? Why so it is. Just a minute, dear.''

The door shut in her face. Allie waited while chains rattled. The door opened once more, swinging wide. ''Come in, Allie. Come in.''

Stepping into the entranceway, Allie briefly explained

the situation. "So," she concluded, "I wanted to let you know where I'd be in case someone, I don't know, needed to get a hold of me or anything."

"Very wise, dear. Very wise. Now, let's make sure I've got the spelling of this young man's name right and the phone number. You just met him, you say? Maybe you'd better call down here every few hours, so I know there's nothing odd going on. You can't pick out the strange ones by their looks, you know. Well, sometimes you can, but not always. I've got a baseball bat in my closet and I won't hesitate to use it. And I've got quite a good swing if I do say so myself. Used to bat cleanup for the company's women's softball team. My, yes, my RBI…that's runs batted in if you're not a follower, dear, why it was impressive."

It took a while but Allie was finally able to get a word in edgewise. She turned down the offer of the bat and convinced Mrs. Klegman to give her until morning to check in. By the time she'd stepped back out into the hall and was on her way upstairs, Allie's ears were ringing. She was also very grateful that Mrs. Klegman's was an efficiency apartment with no room for overnight guests. While very dear, the woman would have had her half-crazed by morning.

Allie knocked briefly on Nate's door. Immediately, it opened.

"What took you so long?"

Her eyes widened in surprise. "Why? Did I have a curfew?"

"No, you didn't have a curfew, smart aleck." Nate ran a hand through his hair in a distracted gesture. "I was just getting worried, that's all."

"Uh-huh. Nate, I'm a big girl. I haven't checked in with anybody since I moved here over a year ago." She thought she heard him mutter something about her father needing his head examined, but that didn't seem to make a lot of sense, so Allie assumed she'd misheard. "Look, do we need to debate this out in the hall or can I come in? I feel kind of silly standing here holding a pillow sack."

Nate was immediately embarrassed. "Oh, sure. Sorry." He eyed the stuffed pillowcase. "What all have you got in there? You don't have an overnighter?"

"Things," Allie replied primly as she stepped past him.

"Things?"

"Yes. Things I need. And yes I have an overnighter, but I used to pack this way for sleepovers when I was a kid. I'm trying to convince myself that this is going to be fun, you know, an adventure, so I don't feel bad about the current condition of my place."

Nate cleared his throat. He knew he was responsible for the condition of her place. She didn't need to rub his nose in it. "I see. Well, okay, that explains it then. Why don't you bring your *things* inside and make yourself at home?"

"Thank you."

"Oh, you're welcome."

They stood in the living room, eyeing each other. Allie had her pillow clutched to her chest. "Where would you like me to put my stuff?"

Nate cleared his throat. Damn, she'd caught him gawking like a schoolboy. He really hated when that happened. "Sorry. Here, let me take that." He reached for the pillowcase. "You'll be in here." Nate gestured to the bedroom doorway. "I'll take the couch."

"You're too tall for the sofa. You're going to be miserable," Allie warned.

Misery was a foregone conclusion. Nate was at a point where he was still putting most of his money back into the business. The sofa was older but still functional. It had developed a few lumps over the past few years. Nothing terminal but Nate knew he'd feel them and his feet would definitely hang out over the edge.

"I'm trying to be a gentleman, okay? Let me."

Allie shrugged and rolled her eyes as she started for the bedroom. Fine. Whatever. She'd tried. She came to a dead stop at the threshold. "It's king-size."

"Yeah, I know," Nate agreed mournfully as he thought of the narrow, lumpy sofa. He was used to sprawling out.

"Why would a single man buy a king-size bed?" Allie immediately blushed. Stupid question. Nate was so handsome, he probably had all kinds of beautiful women coming on to him. He probably threw orgies right there on the bed. *Oh, God, what am I thinking?* "My neighbor, Mrs. Klegman, knows where I am, just so you know."

Nate eyed her curiously. "What is going on in that head of yours?" He waved an erasing hand. "Forget it. I don't think I want to know." He took a breath and assumed a pontificating pose. "I bought a king-size bed because the salesman assured me it was actually easier to move in and out of apartments than a queen or double. King box springs come in two pieces, you know."

"Uh-huh. And it had absolutely nothing to do with the salesperson getting a bigger commission by selling you more."

Nate really hated feeling stupid. "It *was* very easy to move into the bedroom and I'm sure it will be a piece of cake to get out again."

"How much more did he get you for?"

"It *will* be very easy to move. Okay, a few hundred."

Allie laughed and Nate dropped her stuffed pillowcase on the spread. He grinned sheepishly. "You have a nice laugh. Very infectious. I haven't felt much like laughing recently. It's good to hear."

Sighing, Allie said, "Yes, it's been a long day."

"Long week, long month, long year."

"That, too. Still, you've got to keep your sense of humor. If you can't laugh, you might as well shoot yourself."

"Smile and the world smiles with you?"

"And all those other similar platitudes."

Nate slung a companionable arm around her shoulders. "Come on. Let's go have that tea. I hope you remembered the tea bags. We need to wind down."

Allie reached into the pillowcase, felt around a bit and withdrew a packet. "Here we are." With a last look over her shoulder at the lake-sized bed, she left the bedroom for the kitchen. "Let's go brew a pot."

Conversation wasn't exactly free-flowing, but it wasn't hostile, either. Allie could literally feel herself wilting. "I didn't realize how tired I was."

"It's been a rough day."

"Yes it has," Allie agreed fervently.

"Can I get you anything before you turn in? Did you bring your own towel or do you need...damn!"

"What?"

"Towels. My towels are all still sitting in the washing machine down in the laundry room."

"They're probably gone by now."

"Don't start."

Allie shrugged. His towels. His loss. "Fine. Well, I'm going to bed. If you change your mind about the sofa, let me know."

Change his mind? He'd never wanted to sleep on the sofa in the first place. He wasn't going to change his mind. Right from the beginning he'd wanted Allie in his bed. Of course, he wanted to be in there with her. He just wasn't going to give his father that kind of satisfaction.

Chapter Five

The towels were still there. They were also still wet. By the time Nate transferred them to the dryer, pumped the machine full of quarters, got the load started and returned to his apartment, Allie had disappeared behind a closed bedroom door. *His* closed bedroom door. Nate thought he could hear water running.

Allie was in *his* shower, using *his* soap.

Before much longer she would be crawling into *his* bed between *his* sheets.

"Arrgh!"

At least she wouldn't be putting her head down on his pillow. "There's good news," Nate muttered, staring at the closed door. She'd brought her own pillow. Both of his were propped on the sofa waiting for him, so he wouldn't have to wrestle with that mental image. What, did she think he had cooties? She could have used his pillows, he thought perversely. "What is *wrong* with me?" he questioned himself when he found himself staring at his bedroom door.

He'd never found his bedroom door particularly mesmerizing before. What was his problem?

Hell, he knew what his problem was. Tonight, little Allie was behind that portal.

Nate heard the water shut off, then faint humming. He grinned. Allie MacLord was tone-deaf. Moments later, Nate swore he could hear sheets rustling.

What he wouldn't give to open that damn bedroom door and crawl into bed beside Allie. Wouldn't his father just crow if Nate caved after so little time? Heck, not even a full day. A few rotations around a clock, that was all. It certainly wouldn't say much for Nate's willpower, now would it?

Nate closed his eyes and gritted his teeth. *No.* He would not give the old man that kind of satisfaction. He absolutely, positively would not. To say nothing of the fact that Allie would quite probably crown him with something heavy. Even with their brief acquaintance he already knew Allie wasn't the type to jump into bed with a guy she barely knew. No, Allie was far more likely the type to insist on a wedding band before anything good happened between them. But man, that closed door was really getting to him. Determinedly Nate about-faced and marched himself away from the source of temptation and took himself back down to the laundry room where he watched his towels tumble dry.

His father was going to have to try a whole lot harder than this to get Nate to the marriage altar. Yes, indeed, one heck of a whole lot harder. Nate wasn't easy. He was strong. He had the willpower, the personal fortitude and anything else it would take to sneer at any potential Delilah his father chose to put up against him. Of course he did. He made a mental note to add condoms to his shopping list.

Damn, he wanted Allie so bad he was practically shaking with his need.

"Lust," he assured himself, pathetically grateful when the dryer finally beeped. "The mental image of a woman, any woman in your bed is what's doing it to you, that's all. It's been a long dry spell."

Nate pulled towels out of the dryer and stuffed them into the laundry basket. He didn't bother folding them. He was too busy convincing himself that his long dry spell was in no danger of being cut abruptly short; that the tremors in his legs were because of yesterday's workout; that as captain of his boat he'd hit a patch of rough water but was in no danger of foundering. None. The fact that he had to pause outside his apartment door and mentally gird his loins for the struggle ahead—no pun intended—was *not* encouraging.

"This is ridiculous, he muttered when he finally slapped open the door. "She may be woman, but *I* am man. *I* am strong." He really needed to get those condoms.

Untwisting a pair of sweatpants from the tangle of towels, Nate retreated to the guest bath off the kitchen, changed and brushed his teeth. He threw himself on the living room sofa after wrapping himself up in the afghan he kept draped over the couch back. His feet did indeed dangle over the end. The sofa was, in fact, lumpy and narrow even with the back cushions tossed onto the floor. Nate put his hands behind his head and stared up at the ceiling. It was going to be a long night, he suspected. Scratch suspect, he knew it with bone-deep certainty.

Allie rolled from her side to her stomach. Half a minute later she flopped over onto her back. Turning her head, she glared at the bedside clock glowing mean-spiritedly beside her. Two in the morning. She had to face a classroom of fifth-graders at eight-thirty. You couldn't show any sign of weakness in front of a savvy group of inner city kids like that. You had to be on top of things every second of the time spent with them or they'd roll right over you. Walking into her classroom after a restless, sleepless night was an invitation to disaster.

At 2:07 a.m. Allie curled onto her side, away from the clock, trying her umpteen millionth sleeping position. All her tossing and turning had made a twisted train wreck out of the sheets. It was impossible to get comfortable.

"This is ridiculous," she declared, throwing the sheets off and sitting up. She got out of bed and prowled the limited floors space not taken up by Nate's king-size bed. Other than her own agitated breathing, all seemed quiet.

"Maybe some hot cocoa," Allie said. She listened at the door and found herself mildly resentful when she detected no sound in the living area. Evidently she was the only one uneasy with the sleeping arrangements. Nate had evidently conked right out. So much for her worries about her virtue. Mr. Nathaniel Parker was obviously uninterested.

The jerk.

He could have at least made a pass so she would have had the opportunity to tell him where to go.

"Humph." Allie put one hand on the doorknob and gently twisted. If she was quiet, she could probably slip right past Nate and get her hot chocolate. If she was quick and the potion worked, she could maybe get two or three hours of sleep. It wasn't much, but right about now she'd take what she could get and be pathetically grateful for it.

She slipped like a wraith from the bedroom and crept soundlessly past the sofa.

"Where are you going?" asked Nate.

"Don't do that!" Allie shrieked as she jumped. One hand flew to her chest. "Are you trying to give me heart failure?'' She spun around. Nate wasn't even on the sofa. He was standing over by the window peering out into the dark night. ''Why aren't you in bed?''

Nate shrugged. ''Couldn't sleep.''

''Yeah,'' Allie said. ''Me neither.''

''Sorry for scaring you.''

Allie cleared her throat. ''It's okay.''

Nate turned to look at her. ''Where were you going?''

''To the kitchen.'' Allie gestured awkwardly. ''I thought some hot chocolate might help.''

''Ah.'' Nodding sagely, Nate led the way. He flicked on one lone light. Even so, they both had to cover their eyes with a hand.

''Of course, between you scaring me half to death and the bright light, I'm more awake than ever. It may take somebody hitting me over the head with a sledgehammer to put me to sleep now.''

Nate felt a stab of guilt. None of this was Allie's fault. At least on an intellectual level, he understood that. The current ache in an essentially male area that had him nearly doubled over with its intensity was his father's fault, pure and simple. And somehow, he would make his father pay.

Nate opened the refrigerator and pulled out a milk carton. Broodingly he watched Allie pat her chest in an instinctive gesture to calm her heart. It wasn't as if she was wearing a French-cut nightie. It wasn't as if her pajamas were transparent or even translucent, for crying out loud. The woman was wearing sweatpants and an oversize T-shirt, not baby dolls that showed off her legs. Nothing hung off one shoulder or dipped deeply in front to accidentally display anything vital. There was not even a hint of cleavage.

So why did he have an insane urge to thump his own chest a few times to get his heartbeat back under control? Perform a little self-administered CPR?

All right, she obviously wasn't wearing a bra under her shirt. Her nipples were hard and were tenting out her T-shirt the tiniest bit. Big deal. He'd seen nipples before. In the flesh he'd seen them. This was ridiculous. He was thirty, not fifteen.

Were Allie's brown or pink?

"You're spilling."

"What? Oh, yeah, so I am. Hand me the sponge, will you?"

Nate wiped up the milk he'd sloshed and aimed more carefully. "Here. Put these mugs into the microwave, will you? I'll get the cocoa packets."

"You have any marshmallows?"

"It's two-thirty in the morning and you want marshmallows? Yuck. No, I don't. Be grateful I've got hot-chocolate mix."

Allie removed the mugs of heated milk when the microwave dinged. She dumped cocoa mix in and morosely stirred. "Right now I'm having trouble being grateful for much of anything."

"Yeah. I know the feeling."

"No, you can't possibly know what it's like to face thirty-six inner city preadolescents on no sleep. I'm a dead woman."

Nate's head jerked up.

Allie noticed and immediately tried to calm him. "Figuratively speaking. The kids know if they tried anything physical they'd be back in the public schools. They'll just run me ragged."

Nate sipped and banged his mug down. "Ought to make Dad go with you to help out. If he hadn't messed with the garbage disposal, you'd be sound asleep in your own bed right now." And Nate would be asleep in *his* own bed instead of sitting across from a woman he'd just met and all but slavering all over her.

Allie propped her head on her hand and glared balefully at Nate. "What is your problem? I suppose the current economic slowdown is your father's fault as well." She pointed a finger at him. "You know what? You need help. A good shrink might help you get to the root of why you need to transfer blame for everything under the sun to your father. Things happen. Pipes break. You don't appreciate your father. He's a nice guy who obviously cares a great deal about you. He was just trying to help and all you can do is snarl and dump all over him. You ought to be ashamed of yourself."

"What? *What?*" Nate had to steady his cocoa mug. He'd almost knocked it over when he'd recoiled from her attack. "I do not blame the ills of the world on my dad. I only hit him up for the things I can directly trace to his doorstep. Those pipes were fine until he crawled under my sink last night. And if you think otherwise, you're the crazy one, not me." Nate erased his last comment with a hand motion. "No, not crazy, naive."

Allie rolled her eyes. "Naive. Right. I work in the inner city every day but I'm naive. That's a good one."

"Face it. Maybe you're street-smart when it comes to inner city life," he said, although he doubted it, "but you're people stupid. You've been suckered in by my dad's charm. You have no idea what it's like to deal with him on a regular basis so you really shouldn't criticize. I've been a freaking saint up until now. A damned *saint*."

"A damned saint? Isn't that a contradiction in terms?"

"You know what I mean."

"Your problem is you don't know how lucky you are to have a father like him. You could have my father instead."

Nate sat up straight, suddenly alert. "He's not abusive, is he? I mean, he's never hit you or anything?"

"No, no, nothing like that. Most everybody else likes him, in fact. Heck, *I* like him. It's just that since Mom died, he and my brothers, well, let's say I had to move two states away just so I could breathe."

"You mean they're interfering."

"God, yes."

Nate sank back down into his seat. "Let me get this straight. I should be grateful my father loves me enough to interfere in my life on a regular basis, but you get to be resentful of your interfering family? Have I got it right?"

Allie squirmed. "It's not the same. This is different."

Nate crossed his arms over his chest and eyed her consideringly. "Different. Uh-huh. Right."

Allie tried to hold eye contact. She didn't want to be the first to look away. But after a brief stare-down, they both cracked up laughing.

"Man, what are we going to do with them?"

"Let them drive us crazy, I guess." Allie shrugged. "What else is there? We love them."

"Yeah," Nate agreed. "We do." He sighed in a heartfelt way.

Allie tipped up her mug, swallowing the last of her cocoa. "Well, sufficient unto tomorrow are…"

"What?" Nate took the two empty mugs, rose and rinsed them at the sink.

"Uh, I don't know. I can't remember. The woes of tomorrow? Or was that today? The worries of…um…"

He snorted out a laugh. "Great. You're going to have to brush up on your platitudes if you want to get married and have children. Mothers are big on platitudes. My own mom was an absolute champ."

"I'll be a great mother. Maybe I don't remember the

exact wording, but it's something about taking care of today's problem today and worrying about tomorrow's when tomorrow comes.''

Nate set the mugs upside down on the drain board. ''Uh-huh. Guess what? It's almost 3 o'clock. That's a.m. Tomorrow's here and my father will no doubt be showing up later on to start wreaking havoc. Time to worry.''

''I'm sure you're exaggerating,'' Allie declared primly. ''And we still need to get some sleep so I'm not going to fret about it. In fact, I'm going back downstairs. Maybe the floor's dry enough for me to sleep there now.''

''No,'' Nate declared roughly. ''You want your father and brothers to kill me for letting you stay in a trashed apartment by yourself with a door that won't even close all the way? You're staying right here where I can keep an eye on you.''

''Move two states away so you can get a life and what happens? You run right into another warden,'' Allie muttered to herself. ''Go figure.''

''Yeah, go figure.'' Nate pointed in the direction of the bedroom. ''Back to bed, sleeping beauty.''

''Unsleeping beauty,'' she retorted. ''I can't sleep on that bed, Nate. It's too big.''

''Tough,'' he declared rather unsympathetically from Allie's viewpoint.

''Tell you what,'' Allie said. ''Since it's obvious you can't sleep out here, either, I'll take the sofa and you take the bed. At least one of us will get some rest that way.''

Nate immediately cut down that idea, too. ''That won't work. I'm going out and buying a new sofa at the first opportunity,'' he said. ''I never realized how lumpy that one had gotten.'' He thought for a moment. ''Okay, here's what we'll do. We'll both sleep on the bed.''

Allie stared at him in amazement. "Say what? No we won't."

Nate raised one hand as though he was about to tell the truth, the whole truth and nothing but the truth. "I won't try anything. Promise." He wouldn't give his father that kind of pleasure even if it killed him, which it might. And, as previously noted, there were no condoms in the place.

Allie's eyes swiveled between the lump-o-matic sofa and Nate's face. It was hard to read his eyes in the dark. Finally she snatched the afghan off the couch. "You sleep under the sheets and I'll sleep on top."

Nate took her arm to guide her through the now dark living room. "I know that bed and it knows me," he said. "I can sleep on it any old way. You get under the sheets so you'll be as comfortable as possible. Sleeping on top of the sheets won't bother me one bit."

Allie examined his statement for any possible catches. She couldn't think of one. "Okay," she finally allowed. "All right, you can be on top."

Nate about swallowed his tongue. And she wasn't naive? Did she even realize what she'd said? Maybe she was a secret master of double entendre. Maybe she was too shy to come out and ask for it but she really wanted him to...

With a disgusted shake of his head, Nate closed the bedroom door with his foot as they passed through the opening. Yeah, right. Uh-huh. And that would make him the world champion of wishful thinking.

"What side do you want?" Allie asked.

Nate indicated his preference with a tip of his head. "I usually sleep on that side."

"Okay." Allie was agreeable. She doubted she'd get much sleep no matter what side she took. When she'd been little she'd occasionally crawled into bed with an older brother during a particularly violent thunderstorm. But, other than that, her experience with guys was surprisingly limited. She'd been too busy studying and had been heavily into extracurricular stuff as well. She was nervous!

Allie crawled in under the sheets and turned her back to Nate's side, thinking that would somehow lessen the intimacy of what they were doing. Allie held herself perfectly still while she waited for the bouncing of the mattress that would announce Nate's arrival in the bed.

Nate studied the sweet line of Allie's draped back. Was he crazy? Was he out of his freaking mind? When had he gotten into self-abuse? He wanted to go over to the wall and bang his head against it a few times, knock a little common sense back into it. Gingerly, and feeling like a fool, Nate lowered his big body onto the bed. He lay on his back and stacked his hands behind his head. He reminded himself that the torture he was experiencing had been all his own idea. *Your own damn fault, your own damn fault, your...* it was almost mesmerizing, like his own personal mantra.

It was a king-size bed. There was plenty of space between them. Nate hitched himself over, closer to the edge anyway. Maybe the faintly flowery smell he associated with freshly washed female hair wouldn't be so overpowering there. And what the heck kind of soap had he left in his shower that smelled so strongly? Nate wished he could remember the brand because he was never buying it again. The combination of shampoo, soap and essence de woman was killing him here. Killing him.

And he'd done it to himself. *Your own damn fault.*

Just what did that say about his level of intelligence?

He'd spent his afternoon shopping for mattresses with a beautiful woman, then he'd spent the evening discussing sleeping arrangements. He had mattresses and beds on the brain just then and the fragrant scent of woman in his nose. Oh, yeah, he was a dead man.

The only fortunate thing about the whole situation was that Allie had her back to him. If she decided to roll over, though, Nate would be in serious trouble. Not only did he doubt his ability to refrain from grabbing her, but his current condition was both painful and obvious. Nate reached down and adjusted the folds of the afghan he'd covered himself with to provide a little more camouflage, just in case.

Surprisingly, he eventually drifted off, Allie's back still firmly to him.

The blare of the alarm going off at six-thirty had both of them jolting awake.

Nate's eyes were wide-open. Adrenaline coursed through his body and he clutched Allie to him without realizing what he was doing. "What! What is it?"

"Oh, God, it's morning. How can it be morning?"

"Are we on fire? What's happening?"

"Shh, no it's okay. I brought my clock up with me. It's just my alarm."

Nate ran a hand over his face. "Holy smoke, I just lost ten years off my life. You wake up to that thing every morning? I'm amazed you haven't succumbed to heart failure."

"Well, the thing is I sleep pretty deeply and…oh my God."

"What now? What?"

"Nothing." If Nate hadn't noticed anything amiss, Allie certainly wasn't going to enlighten him.

"Don't nothing me. It must be something or you wouldn't have…oh." Nate manfully cleared his throat. It felt so natural, he was just then noticing that Allie's head was pillowed on his shoulder, her body not only curled up at his side, but practically bound to him with a twist of knotted sheets. One of her legs covered his thigh, her knee nestled warmly in his groin and her arm draped over his chest, her fingers burrowing in his chest hair. And even though Nate had one arm around Allie's shoulders, anchoring her close, it hadn't been his doing, thank God. Allie was the one who had crossed the invisible boundary line. She was well and truly on his side of the bed. "Uh, here, let me help you, um, untangle yourself."

Allie slapped his helpful hands away. "I can do it, I can do it." Sometime during the night Allie must have tried to kick the sheets and blanket off and snuggled up to Nate for her warmth instead. The man certainly radiated heat. Only problem was, she was good and solidly caught up against him, heck make that *on* him in a solid twist of sheets. Allie hoped like crazy he'd been too sleepy to realize where her hand—and knee, had been. Or where his had landed when he'd first tried to help her. "This is only totally mortifying."

"Don't be silly. Think of it as an act of charity."

Allie stopped struggling with the sheets. "What?"

Now that Nate was more awake, he began to relax. Allie didn't want his help, so he stacked his hands behind his head and let her struggle. If only he was into bondage, why he'd be getting quite a kick out of this. Her struggles to free herself had Allie rubbing against him in a rather sensual body massage. "Seriously. Men have fragile egos, you know."

Allie snorted. "Yeah, right."

"We do! And think how you've helped build mine up. I feel ever so much better about myself now that I know I'm irresistible to the opposite sex."

"Oh, please. Spare me." Allie rolled her eyes as she tugged at the unyielding mess she'd made. "A guy who looks like you. Spare me the pity party. Like there was ever any doubt in your mind.''

Nate laughed, thoroughly enjoying himself. ''Whatever. Come on, let me give you a hand.''

''It's just that I don't trust that ha…there, I've got it. I'm free.'' Allie rolled to her own side of the bed.

Nate immediately missed the warmth of her body. He sighed. Heck, he ought to be grateful. Now that he thought about it, with where her knee had been, why she could have unmanned him when the alarm had gone off. ''I suppose we ought to get up.''

''It's early. Try and go back to sleep.''

Nate rolled his eyes. Yeah, right. Like that was going to happen. He was lucky his heart was still in his chest rather than flopping around on the floor next to the bed.

''I'm the one that's got to get going. Stay.''

She should have thought of that before she'd set an alarm with the power to wake the dead. Reluctantly Nate sat up and swung his feet to the floor. He scratched his chest and stretched. ''Nope, I'm awake now, might as well get moving.'' Nate squinted at the clock. ''Although this is rather obscenely early. You always get up at this time?'' Please say yes, he thought. It would mean their biorhythms didn't match. He'd read somewhere that was important. Probably the dentist waiting room. Why did doctors always have such odd reading material in their waiting rooms? Somebody ought to do a study. At any rate, the point was it was hard to get it on if you were asleep when your partner was up and vice versa.

''It takes me a while to get to work,'' Allie said apologetically. ''Remember I told you. The Kennedy and Dan Ryan can be a mess and then there's the drive through Englewood. Fifty-ninth has a stoplight practically every corner.''

"Are you sure you're going to be safe?" Nate asked, concern growing as she described her route. Englewood was about as rough as it got.

"That's why school starts so early," Allie said, shuffling around the end of the bed as she rolled her head, working out the kinks in her neck. "The bad guys are still asleep after a night of raising Cain."

"I'm surprised your father allows you to teach in such a bad area. Even if he's only half as protective as you say he is, I'm surprised."

"I'm twenty-eight. What can he do? And, if you'll remember, that's why I moved."

"So you didn't have to deal with the lectures."

"Right. Now I only have to deal with them Sunday afternoons during my weekly call home."

Nate twisted on the bed so he could see her as they talked. He immediately regretted it. Allie touched her toes, then stretched with her arms crossed up over her head and leaned from side to side. Her T-shirt pulled up and her sweatpants hung on her hipbones, which meant her belly button was exposed.

Who'd have thought belly buttons could be so cute? Allie's was downright adorable and Nate's body immediately twitched to attention.

Nate blew out a breath in disgust. Man, there he went again. Was this going to be a permanent condition when he was around Allie? Hell, he was thirty years old, surely capable of a little more self-control than this.

His body disagreed.

Nate sighed and rolled out of bed. He'd heard cold showers were supposed to be good for this condition. He'd never bothered to check the hypothesis before. It sounded distinctly unappealing. One of those cases where the cure was worse than the problem. This morning, however, Nate found himself unwilling to embarrass Allie. Working where she did, Allie had probably seen and heard a lot worse than Nate himself, but there was still something he might call sweet about her, if it didn't sound so sappy.... "I'm gonna take a shower," he announced, keeping his back to her.

"That's all right. I took one last night."

"I know." He'd heard the water, imagined her standing naked under the spray, her head tipped back as the cascading water slicked her wet hair back. There he went again. "Yeah, I know." Nate drew a breath. "So I'll go jump in myself. There's another bathroom up front."

"Yep. Same place as mine."

"Oh, right. We've got similar layouts. How could I forget?" Nate ran his hand through his hair. Man, chances were real good he had bed head. Allie was probably laughing behind the back he was so carefully keeping to her. "Okay, so you know where it is. If you wouldn't mind using the other bathroom to put on your makeup and all the other guck women seem to feel is essential and takes them *forever,* I can get a shower in sometime today."

Allie rolled her eyes. "Fine. But it only takes me ten minutes to put on makeup."

"Right."

"It's true, you'll see."

Nate really wasn't interested in arguing with her. When you're right, you're right, after all. He had a more pressing problem to take care of. With a grimace of distaste—Nate was a man who liked his creature comforts, after all—he went to turn on the cold water.

By the time Nate had shivered through his shower, shaved, glopped the man's hairstyling product du jour on his head and dressed, close to half an hour had ticked by. He grabbed a tie from his closet and dragged his goosebump ridden carcass into the kitchen area and stopped cold.

Allie had beaten him. She was dressed for work in a crisp, cuffed pair of navy slacks and a stylish sweater set. Her auburn hair was in tousled curls around her face. She had low-heeled pumps on her feet. Allie was already seated and eating a bowl of cereal.

Nate gestured to her wrinkle-free outfit. "You didn't have that jammed into your pillowcase when you came up last night."

"No. I ran downstairs and changed. I brought up some of my favorite cereal to share. Want some?"

She'd beaten him. Nate couldn't believe it. "What about your makeup? You didn't put any on, did you? That's why you were so fast getting out here. I don't see any guck on your face."

Allie fluttered her eyelashes at him. "You're not supposed to see it. Makeup is supposed to be subtle for day wear. And, yes, I do have some on. See?" She leaned forward and closed her eyes so he could inspect her lids.

Nate immediately reared backward. What, was she crazy? Get that close to a man smelling all sweet like that and picture pretty the way she was, you were asking for trouble. Asking for it.

"Damn," Nate muttered. He wished he knew who had started that rumor about the effectiveness of cold showers. He'd sue their butts off because he'd *frozen* his off for nothing.

Hell's bells.

Chapter Six

Nate's second cup of coffee had cooled unnoticed. He had his shirtsleeves literally and figuratively rolled up and he was engrossed in the sheaves of paperwork he'd dealt into—piled across the surface of his desktop—by the time Jared strolled in at eight o'clock.

Jared walked right by Nate's open door, stopped and backed up again to stare. "What're you doing here?" he asked, looking bewildered.

Nate made a production of checking the nameplate on his desk. "I believe I work here."

"Ha-ha. You're never on time. What's the matter? Couldn't sleep?"

"Shut up," Nate growled. He'd slept. Some.

"Hey, I'm not complaining. You always stay later than I do, so it all works out. It's just weird is all. What's up?"

"Let it go, man. I'm here early today, period. There's nothing more to tell." A whole lot of nothing. He'd no doubt be feeling one heck of a lot better this morning if there'd been...something. But there hadn't been and Nate was not about to go into an explanation of why he'd had a restless night. He was becoming resigned to the fact that even *thinking* about Allie would probably put his body into an uncomfortable state. Furthermore, even if he was inclined to try another cold shower, they didn't have the facilities there in the office. Heck, to use a bathroom at all, they had to leave their office and go out into the common area of their floor of the office building.

Jared held his hands up in a surrendering gesture. "Okay, fine. Be that way. I'll just stay out of your way the rest of the day. But, Nate?"

"What?"

"Let me handle the customer calls today, all right? In your present mood you'll just scare business away and we need it. You should have slept in."

Nate wondered what the penalty was for murdering business partners. Was it considered a white-collar crime since theirs was a white-collar business? He'd read somewhere that white-collar criminals seldom did actual time. It might be worth it. He muttered to himself for a moment.

"Jared?"

His partner stuck his head back in the doorway. "What?"

"Get back in here."

Jared stayed where he was, warily eyeing Nate. "Why? You gonna bite my head off again? I'm telling you, man, you need an attitude adjustment this morning."

"I need to talk to you for a minute." The pencil he'd begun to twirl between the fingers of his right hand broke free and flew across the room.

Jared watched the flight of the small missile. "I don't know, Nate."

"You'll be safe." Nate held up one hand. "Promise."

Jared hitched up his trousers and came in. "Okay, but

at the first sign of physical hostility, I'm out of here. I can't stand the sight of blood, especially my own.'' Jared drew up a chair to the opposite side of Nate's desk and sat down. ''What's up?''

Nothing that could be mentioned in polite company.

Nate slumped back into his chair, tipped his head back and closed his eyes. Eight o'clock in the morning and they already felt gritty. It was going to be a long day. ''Remember when I had to leave early yesterday?''

''Yeah. You didn't feel you had to make up for that, did you? You know you more than pull your own weight around here and really, your father doesn't bug me *that* much. It would only be fair for you to be the one to fix up the books if your dad screws them up, of course, but…''

''Jared, would you please be quiet and just listen for a minute?''

Jared folded his hands in his lap and straightened in his chair. ''Go for it.''

At the end of his recitation, Nate opened his eyes and sat up. ''And that's about it except that I'm thinking about running away from home because I don't want to go back tonight and see what kind of disaster he's made of Allie's repairs. At this rate I could be sharing my bed with her for months.''

Jared looked at him oddly. ''And this would be a bad thing because…? I mean, you did say she had a great body, that she was seriously cute and everything, right? Come on, what are you complaining about? Hell, she can come stay with me. I wouldn't mind being noble and sharing *my* bed with her.''

''Jared,'' Nate growled warningly.

''But I'll want to see a picture first,'' Jared stipulated. ''Your idea of hot and mine could be different, after all. Remember? You thought that one actress, you remember, the blonde? The one with the big—'' Jared gestured to his chest ''—in whatever the name of that movie was you told me to go see was a babe.''

''She was.''

''Not only was she a dog, but the movie stank, too.''

''What are you talking about? That was a great…'' Nate shook his head. ''I can't believe I'm letting you sidetrack me like this. Could we stick to the topic, please?''

Jared shrugged. ''I just don't see the problem. You're being forced to sleep with some totally hot babe. My heart bleeds for you. Instead of bitching about your dad, I'd think you'd be grateful. Heck, I'd be praying for a few more disasters if you could get a guarantee they'd have this kind of outcome. Hey, could you maybe ask if she's got any available friends? Maybe we could double-date or something. Have an overnight party,'' Jared offered with a slightly malicious grin.

''Okay, you know what? Just forget it. You obviously don't have the first clue about what's going on here and I can't explain it any better. Just…go be productive or something.''

''Sheesh,'' Jared muttered as he pushed himself out of the chair. ''Try to give a guy some advice and…forget the attitude adjustment, Nate. You need the whole enchilada— a complete personality transplant.''

''Out.''

''I'm going, I'm going.''

Jared was an idiot. Nate couldn't believe he'd been dumb enough to attempt to go into business with him. It was amazing that the fledgling company hadn't gone belly-up the first week. Nate picked up a pencil and began to run it down a column of numbers.

Where was Jared's sympathy for Allie, hmm? Where was that? Poor little thing comes home probably all wrecked

Silhouette ROMANCE®

DIANA PALMER

MERCENARY
WOMAN
SOLDIERS OF FORTUNE

We'd like to send you **2 FREE** books and a surprise gift to introduce you to Silhouette Romance®. Accept our special offer today and

Get Ready for a totally Refreshing Experience!

HOW TO QUALIFY:

1. With a coin, carefully scratch off the silver area on the card at right to see what we have for you—2 FREE BOOKS and a FREE GIFT—ALL YOURS! ALL FREE!

2. Send back the card and you'll receive two brand-new Silhouette Romance® novels. These books have a cover price of $3.99 each in the U.S. and $4.50 each in Canada, but they are yours to keep absolutely free!

3. There's no catch. You're under no obligation to buy anything. We charge nothing—ZERO—for your first shipment and you don't have to make any minimum number of purchases—not even one!

4. The fact is, thousands of readers enjoy receiving books by mail from the Silhouette Reader Service™ Program. They enjoy the convenience of home delivery…they like getting the best new novels at discount prices, BEFORE they're available in stores…and they love their *Heart to Heart* subscriber newsletter featuring author news, horoscopes, recipes, book reviews and much more!

5. We hope that after receiving your free books you'll want to remain a subscriber. But the choice is yours—to continue or cancel, any time at all. So why not take us up on our invitation with no risk of any kind. You'll be glad you did!

SPECIAL FREE GIFT!

We can't tell you what it is…but we're sure you'll like it! A FREE gift just for giving the Silhouette Reader Service™ Program a try!

Visit us online at www.eHarlequin.com

Your FREE Gifts include:
- 2 Silhouette Romance® books!
- An exciting mystery gift!

Scratch off the silver area to see what the Silhouette Reader Service™ Program has for you.

Silhouette®
Where love comes alive®

YES!
I have scratched off the silver area above. Please send me the **2 FREE** books and gift for which I qualify. I understand I am under no obligation to purchase any books, as explained on the back and on the opposite page.

315 SDL DU3Z   215 SDL DU4H

FIRST NAME   LAST NAME

ADDRESS

APT.#   CITY

STATE/PROV.   ZIP/POSTAL CODE

©2001 HARLEQUIN ENTERPRISES LTD. ® and ™ are trademarks owned by Harlequin Books S.A. used under license.

(S-R-08/03)

THE SILHOUETTE READER SERVICE™ PROGRAM—Here's how it works:

Accepting your 2 free books and gift places you under no obligation to buy anything. You may keep the books and gift and return the shipping statement marked "cancel." If you do not cancel, about a month later we'll send you 6 additional books and bill you just $3.34 each in the U.S., or $3.80 each in Canada, plus 25¢ shipping & handling per book and applicable taxes if any.* That's the complete price and — compared to cover prices of $3.99 each in the U.S. and $4.50 each in Canada — it's quite a bargain! You may cancel at any time, but if you choose to continue, every month we'll send you 6 more books, which you may either purchase at the discount price or return to us and cancel your subscription.

*Terms and prices subject to change without notice. Sales tax applicable in N.Y. Canadian residents will be charged applicable provincial taxes and GST.

If offer card is missing write to: Silhouette Reader Service, 3010 Walden Ave., P.O. Box 1867, Buffalo NY 14240-1867

DETACH AND MAIL CARD TODAY!

BUSINESS REPLY MAIL

FIRST-CLASS MAIL   PERMIT NO. 717-003   BUFFALO, NY

POSTAGE WILL BE PAID BY ADDRESSEE

SILHOUETTE READER SERVICE
3010 WALDEN AVE
PO BOX 1867
BUFFALO NY 14240-9952

NO POSTAGE
NECESSARY
IF MAILED
IN THE
UNITED STATES

TERRY ESSIG   97

from a day in the bowels of the city and what happens? Some madman trashes her apartment and she's forced to sleep with a virtual stranger.

When you thought about it, Nate and his dad were lucky she hadn't had a nervous breakdown or gone hysterical on them. "She could have, you know. Dad was just damn lucky, that's all. But no, Jared wants to turn Allie's trials and tribulations into some kind of damn overnight party. Oh, and does she have a friend whose apartment we can trash so Jared can have a playmate, too?" Disgustedly Nate pushed the one paper he'd been working on aside and started on the next. What the heck was he doing? Oh, yeah, looking for glaring discrepancies in the addition of the numbers. He started the pencil down the paper.

"She's lucky I wasn't some mad rapist."

The pencil stopped.

Allie *was* lucky.

"Humph. Woman needs a keeper. My God, I could have been anybody." Which made absolutely no sense at all. He could have been anybody? "You know what I mean." Yes he did. "Still, she shouldn't have...I could have...hmm." Nate began to weave a complex fantasy of the things he *could* have tried. Had he been any other kind of guy.

He snapped to when the phone rang. "Sheesh," he muttered, and ran a hand over his face after a brief conversation with a client. "I know cold showers don't work. So what would?" Nate tried to bury himself in his work once more, but his thoughts continued to circle around to Allie. "I'm just going to have to watch out for her myself," he ended up deciding. "It's only right, after the way we've put her out," he declared virtuously. "And I'll keep my hands to myself. It'll be hard because the woman is seriously hot, but she's obviously putting her trust in me and I can't let her down."

Oh, man. He was one dead duck.

The phone rang again. Nate picked it up. His father's voice sounded in his ear. Uh-oh. "Dad? Why are you calling? Something else has gone wrong, hasn't it?"

"Well, now—"

"What? What? Don't prolong the agony. I can't take it. Just spit it out."

"Well, now—"

"Dad!"

"I'm getting to it, Mr. Impatient, I'm getting to it." Ted cleared his throat. "Now, Nate," he began.

Nate's forehead clunked down onto his desktop. He left it there. "Yeah?"

"It could be I might have accidentally tipped over a gallon of paint onto Allie's bedroom carpeting.

Nate's shoulders slumped. "Dad?"

"Yes, son?"

"How does one *accidentally* dump a gallon of paint on the floor? That's kind of a large quantity, isn't it?" A new thought occurred to him. His head popped off the desktop and his eyes narrowed suspiciously. "Dad? What were you doing with a gallon of paint? You couldn't have repaired the ceiling and been ready to paint that quickly."

"Yeah, well…"

Was it possible his father could be doing any of this on purpose? Surely not even his father could have foreseen the consequences of messing with his garbage disposal. Could he? Of course there was always the possibility His Deviousness was simply taking advantage of serendipity. Maybe the garbage disposal thing *had* simply sort of happened, one of those things, and Ted had chosen to run with it to further his own ends. Man, talk about low! Nate himself would never sink to such depths. Except for maybe…now.

But his father would have only himself to blame if Nate chose that low road at this point, Nate rationalized. "Dad?"

"Nate, I swear, this was strictly an accident."

"Uh-huh. Exactly how did this accident happen to occur?"

"I was trying to save some time. I know how you value your privacy," Ted declared virtuously. "That's why you moved out of the house, right? And I want to get Allie out of your place as quickly as I can. Don't want the neighbors talking, you know. Uh, to say nothing of the fact we don't want her finding out all your little…peccadilloes just yet. A man's got to keep some mystery, after all. I'm not saying you're not a good-looking guy or that some woman won't be lucky to get you. It's just that if they find out you can hit a basket easily from past the three point line but can't make the hamper with your dirty socks and your silverware drawer's a mess even though you've got an organizer right there, well then, the shine on your appeal gets a bit tarnished. You know what I'm saying? Women are funny about stuff like that. For some reason it bothers them if your underwear's a tad gray 'cuz it's too much bother for you to separate the lights from the darks. It's just all around better if you've got them hooked *before* little stuff like that comes to light."

Nate was horrified to discover he was prone to facial tics. "The paint, Dad. Tell me about the paint."

Ted cleared his throat. "Yeah, well anyway, while I was waiting for things to dry out a little more—I'm here to tell you, it must have gotten really soaked up there. I'm surprised your own flooring hasn't warped. Subflooring, too, for that matter."

Nate grimaced and pressed a hand against his cheek to slow down the tic. He supposed he'd have to pay more attention when he got home and check out the evenness of the floor. He'd been so concerned with Allie's place, he'd given his own only a cursory glance. Delightful. That certainly gave him something to look forward to at the end of the day. "Let's stick to the point here, Dad. The paint. How did the paint get on Allie's carpeting?"

"Yes, well, I was thinking of things I could do while I was waiting, you know? So I thought I'd pick up the paint for the ceiling, have it all there and ready to go. So I went back to the hardware store."

"Yeah?"

"I thought it would be easy. Her ceiling's white, right?"

"White, right." How hard could that be? Leave it to his father to complicate a simple issue.

"Do you have any idea how many ceiling whites there are?"

Nate used his free hand to massage the now aching base of his skull. Forget the twitch. He wouldn't have to worry about it if his head fell off. "No, Dad, how many?"

"A lot. One whole heck of a lot. Entire brochures full. So I just kind of went eeny meeny miney moe and grabbed one."

"Okay, I'm with you so far, Dad."

"I wanted to see how close I was with my match."

"So you…" Nate waited for his father to fill in the blank. The suspense was killing him. Heck, maybe he was already dead and living in an alternate world. It was beginning to feel that way.

"So I took off the paint can lid so I could climb up and hold it up to the ceiling. For a comparison. The bottom side of the lid gets covered with paint when they shake up the can for you, you know."

"Uh-huh." The tic was picking up speed. His was going to be the most well exercised cheek in town.

"Well, her bedroom's kind of crowded. There really

wasn't room to set a stepladder up properly so I just kind
of leaned it against a wall.''

He could see what was coming. It was an OSHA, Oc-
cupational Safety and Health Administration, nightmare.
''The ladder fell, didn't it? Did you hurt yourself, Dad? I
know you hate doctors, but if you're hurt...''

''Nah, I didn't take a tumble or anything. The ladder just
kind of slipped a little bit. I managed to grab onto the
dresser and stabilize myself, but in the process I kind of
knocked the open paint can off the end of the dresser. Uh,
it didn't land right side up.''

No. That would have been asking a lot. Murphy's Law
still ruled.

''One good thing. Not much got on the dresser itself.''

Oh, God. Nate didn't want to think about how much
qualified as not much in his father's estimation.

''Mostly it's the carpet. Just a little bit spattered on the
bed linens, things like that.''

Oh, well then. As long as it was only a little bit on the
bed linens and dresser, that was all right. Nate's brain had
reached its limits and went numb. Damn. *Not much* and *a
little bit*. He could learn to hate phrases like that. Oh, well,
What was done was done and Nate was becoming more or
less inured to disaster. ''So, Dad, don't leave me in suspense here. Did the paint match?''

''What?''

''Did you guess right? Does the paint you bought match
the white of the ceiling?''

''Nate? You all right, son? You sound kind of strange.''

''Do I?''

''To tell you the truth, I figured you'd be kind of angry
right about now.''

''Did you?'' What would be the point of being angry?

His life had gone so far south, it was laughable and that's just what Nate did. He laughed.

"Nate? I'll be right over. You hang on, son. I'm on my way."

That kind of threat made Nate sit up and take notice. "No. No, you stay there, Dad. I'll stay here, you stay there." Oh, God, get a grip, Nate, old boy. You're getting hysterical. "Just, uh, get as much off the dresser as you can. Get it wiped down quickly before it dries. It was latex, right? It should be all right."

His father was silent on the other end.

"Uh, Dad? It *was* latex."

"Now, Nate, you know I'm kind of from the old school when it comes to paint. You just can't beat oil based paint for durability to my way of thinking."

Damn. Oil based. Double damn. "Wipe the furniture down quickly, Dad. Get any drips off the wall that you see before they harden. No way you can mop up an entire gallon out of the carpet, especially since it's oil based. We'll have to replace that and the sheets as well, I suppose. I'll have a look when I get there around six."

"You're not coming right over?"

What could he possibly accomplish by running right over other than delaying the slitting of his own wrists for a few more hours, which would be a good thing to his way of thinking? "No, Dad, I've got too much to do here. I left early yesterday, remember? Do what you can and I'll figure out what our next step should be when I get there, all right?"

"I'll put the linens to soak."

"Fine, Dad. You do that." Not that it would do any good.

Nate did his best to concentrate the rest of the day, but it was tough going. His thoughts tumbled and careened from pillar to post. Allie in his bed. His father flooding Allie's apartment. Allie in his bed. The Ansom contract. Allie in his bed. White paint on Allie's pink carpet. Take a guess on his next thought.

"Argh!" Nate grabbed his own hair and yanked. "Ow!"

Finally it was five-thirty. Nate felt he'd put in a full forty-hour work week since he'd arrived early that morning. Nate grabbed his briefcase and stood. The never-ending day was over. The sun was actually thinking about sinking even if it hadn't gotten around to actually performing the act.

But did he really want to go home?

He sat back down. Leaving meant facing the farcical comedy his personal life had become. "Damn." Allie was there by now. She'd seen the paint all over her girly-girl pink bedroom carpet, on her dresser and on her bed linens. How could he face her? "The Nelson contract could use another going-over. I should probably double-check those numbers one more time. Just to, you know, be sure."

Coward.

"All right! Fine! I'll go home and face her. But I'm warning you, if she cries, I'm going to—what?" If Allie was in tears, Nate would what?

Panic. Freak. Probably start to blubber himself. And if that wasn't a revolting moment of self-revelation, Nate didn't know what was.

"Shoot." He took a deep breath, picked up his briefcase and headed for the door. Forward momentum. That's what was needed. Once begun, momentum was easier to maintain. It was some kind of law of physics. Sure.

Nate managed to get himself home. He got himself out of the car, into the building and up to the second floor. He kind of stalled out at Allie's condo door. "Be brave," he told himself. "You don't hear any shrieking, do you? The worst is probably over. Probably just a question of mopping

up tears at this point.'' Oh, God. Tears were the worst. And
Allie, who'd put up such a brave front yesterday, well, *her*
tears would be worse than the worst.

Nate leaned his head against the doorjamb. He took several deep, fortifying breaths. Finally he gave the door a
nudge. He was met with silence.

Damn. Allie was probably in the bedroom, staring at the
ruin of her pretty pink flower bower of a bedroom, leaking
slow silent tears down her cheeks. Her chin would still be
up because Allie was no coward—hadn't she taken last
night with total equanimity?—and her tears would sort of
drip onto her chest forming an ever-widening damp circle.
Oh, man, this was worse than the worst of the worst. This
was the pits.

Nate edged into the small entrance foyer and glanced into
the kitchen before he proceeded into the living room. He
was just about to call out when he heard her.

''Ted, I want you to stop this right now.''

Uh-oh. Sounded like sweet little Allie had had it. She
was laying into his father. There was definite impatience in
Allie's voice when she responded.

''It's not like you did it on purpose. It was an *accident*,
okay? And accidents happen. Nobody's to blame. You were
trying to help. I understand that.''

What was this? Allie wasn't going to take his father's
head off and hand it to him on a platter? She was attempt-
ing to *comfort* him? Make him feel all better? For virtually
single-handedly destroying her home?

What, Allie was some kind of freaking saint?

Nate couldn't help but wonder what it would take to get
the woman riled. Would his father have to blow up the
building? She'd probably get mad then—but only if he'd
done it with malice aforethought.

''You couldn't have known that you were only setting

the stain when you tried to clean up. Just calm down. Nate'll be here any minute. Then we'll get everything straightened out.''

If Nate had been closer to the wall, he'd have banged his head against it for sure. Wait, no. With his kind of luck, he'd put a hole in the wall and his head would get stuck. Besides, Allie had had enough of her place destroyed by the Parker family. He was going to have to suck it in. Self-control. Restraint. Nate had always thought he'd had them in spades. Boy, had he ever been wrong. Still he reached for reservoirs Nate hadn't known he possessed. Instead of entering the bedroom like a screaming maniac—his first impulse—he calmly pushed the door more widely open and said, ''Allie? Dad? I'm—dear Lord!''

The flower bower had taken a direct hit from a paint bomb. It looked like one of those places kids went to have paint wars.

Nate's eyes widened as he took in the destruction. Who'd have thought you could squeeze that amount of liquid into a can that size? ''Allie, I don't know what to s—''

Allie was wildly gesticulating behind his father's back. It was obvious she wanted him to well, shut up, to not hurt his father's feelings.

She *was* a freaking saint.

''Your dad's a little worried that you're going to be up-set, Nate.''

''Is he now?'' Nate continued to look around in amazement. In what may have been a misguided attempt to clean up, Ted had somehow managed to smear paint everywhere. ''Can't imagine why he'd think that, can you?''

''He couldn't find any rags and the sponge he was using got saturated fairly quickly.''

''I'll bet it did.''

"It ended up with paint sort of spread, well, everywhere."

"So I see."

Allie gave him her most winning smile. "I told him you and I would fix things right up."

"Will we?" Nate asked. "I'd like to know h—oh, hell," he bit off in disgust at more of Allie's shushing motions. "Of course. You and I will take care of things. No problem." But he still wanted to know how. What was he, some kind of miracle worker? But Allie was right. No point in making his father feel worse. "Don't worry about it, Dad. We'll have things straightened out in no time."

"Nate, no, that wouldn't be right."

"Oh, it would. Really it would." Especially considering the alternative. His father was going to feel compelled to keep trying to fix things, which would send Allie's condo into a downward spiral that would probably only end with the collapse of the entire building.

"Dad, here's what I think you should do."

"Yes?"

He was thinking, he was thinking.

"Tomorrow you should…uh, go to school with Allie."

Allie straightened up at that. "What?"

"You make use of parent volunteers, don't you? Most schools do."

"Well, sure. There's a lot of busy work they can handle that's very helpful. Correcting papers, changing bulletin boards, helping a student who needs some one on one, but…"

"See, Dad? This is a great idea. You go with Allie in the morning. She's under a lot of stress right now. Difficult kids in her classroom, water, paint, you know. You could go and work with some of the kids who are having trouble with whatever—math, English. You'd be good at that. You helped me with homework all the time, remember?''

"Well, sure, but—''

Nate was ruthless. His father was not going to be left on his own anywhere near Allie's condo if Nate could help it. Nate rolled right over any objections. "No, really. You'll see. This'll be great. You help out at her school during the day, then, on the way home, take Allie to the um, mall! Yes, you two can pick out new sheets and a new bedspread.''

"Soaking them in cold water set the paint,'' Allie had to admit. "I don't think we're going to get it out at this point.''

"There you go,'' Nate said. "You heard it straight from the source. The old linens are unsalvageable. The least we can do is help her replace them. I've got to go into work myself, but I'll call a flooring place and make an appointment for them to come out and see about replacing the carpeting.''

"We probably shouldn't replace the carpeting until after the ceiling is done. In case there's, you know, another accident or something.''

He'd already thought of that possibility and was running one step in front of his father. His father didn't have to know that, however, and he doubted the situation would last long anyway. His old man was tricky. "Right,'' Nate said simply. "Good idea, Dad. We'll just get an estimate on the carpet and I'll call around in the morning. Maybe I can find somebody to fix the ceiling in a hurry.''

"But we've already bought all the stuff. I'd still like to try—''

"You're going to be pretty busy, Dad. Why don't we take a wait-and-see kind of attitude here? Give this a couple of days. I know I'll feel a lot better if Allie's got someone else in the car with her while she's driving through those questionable neighborhoods.''

Ted's eyes narrowed as he considered his options. He looked longingly at the ceiling. ''I've always wanted to try my hand at home maintenance kind of things but I was always too busy at work. By the time I'd get around to something, your mother would have already had people out and the problem was taken care of.'' Ted sighed. ''But you could be right. I know I'll feel better if Allie's not alone in the car. If you can't find anyone right away, I could get back to this come the weekend. It ought to be good and dry by then.''

Nate closed his eyes on a prayer of gratitude. He'd bought himself two days at any rate. Surely he'd think of something, although God only knows what, by Friday. Heck, he'd settle for just containing the damage at this point. ''Okay, good, that's settled then. Uh…'' What he needed to do here was lose his father for a while so he could find out how upset Allie really was. Granted she was putting up a brave front and he owed her big for that, but being a woman, well they liked to be held and stuff. She probably needed a good cry. Nate grimaced at the thought. Well, he could handle it. In all likelihood it wouldn't kill him to hold her while she cried. Allie deserved that much.

''Tell you what, Dad. I need to change and Allie probably has a few things she wants to get done as well. Why don't you go to the store and pick us all up something for dinner? We can meet upstairs in say, an hour? We'll put a meal together and take the night off from all of this.'' Nate gestured to the disaster around him. ''We'll play Scrabble or something.''

His father immediately declined. ''No, no.'' Ted held up his hand in denial of the offer. ''If we're not going to do any work here, I'm going to haul my sorry carcass on

home. A couple of my favorite shows are on tonight. I think
I'll park myself in front of the TV, give you two some
alone time.''

No. Nate froze. There was no way his father could have
planned this to throw him together with Allie again. Nobody was that sneaky and devious. Impossible.

But whether by machination or accident, he was spending his evening with Allie while he comforted her, knowing
full well in advance he'd probably be unmanned by her
tears and end up with a soggy shirtfront while cradling her
soft body up against his, his arms around her, breathing in
her heavenly scent....

Chapter Seven

Ted cleared out in short order, leaving Nate and Allie alone in her bedroom, a situation that sounded a lot better than it actually was. Nate had one hand in his pants pocket while he massaged the back of his neck with the other. "I don't know," he said while he rocked on his heels. "This little vignette kind of strikes me as a microcosm of my life lately."

"What do you mean?" Allie wistfully eyed her paint-spattered bedspread. It was only a couple of months old. The tag with the washing instructions was still crisp and legible.

"Here I am alone with a beautiful woman in her boudoir. Close your eyes and think about it," Nate directed. "The possibilities are endless. At least they should be endless. If I were the kind of guy who indulged in locker-room kind of talk, man, the other guys would be green with envy. Last night a total babe slept with me after knowing me for only a few hours and now, here we are, rendezvousing in her bedroom the very next afternoon. Describe the scene to anyone else and what would they assume? Afternoon delight, that's what.''

Allie stared at him in amazement. Nate's eyes were closed. His face wore a wistful expression.

''Without lying or exaggerating, I would have them so convinced that I was a complete stud.'' Nate sighed at the mental imagery.

''What did you add to your coffee when you took your afternoon break?'' she wanted to know. ''I think somebody substituted something funky for the sugar. Either that or your office's cream has gone bad.''

''But then, you know, I open my eyes and wham! Reality hits.'' Nate opened his eyes and he gazed around. Sure enough, the mess was still there. It wasn't simply a bad dream. ''On the surface,'' Nate continued, ''my life sounds ideal. I work for myself. I own my own condo. My father is devoted to my happiness and there's a gorgeous woman warming my bed at night. But you know what?''

''What?''

Nate waggled a finger at her. ''It would only work if the guys I was trying to impress knew absolutely nothing about me. Because the reality of my life? Well, it bites, you know?''

Allie tried hard to be a the-glass-is-half-full kind of person, but she was hard-pressed to argue with Nate's interpretation of the past two days. The glass was definitely looking half-empty right about then.

Nate opened up his arms, held them wide. ''And I'm a jerk. Thinking only of myself. Allie, I am so, so sorry.''

She sniffled. She couldn't help herself and wasn't that embarrassing in the extreme? She hated weepy females.

''Come here,'' Nate said.

''No,'' Allie said, swiping at her nose with the back of her hand. ''I'm okay. Really,'' she insisted. ''I'm all right.''

"Come on," Nate encouraged, arms still open.

Oh, damn, she was going to cry. Allie looked around, everywhere but at Nate. "It's just that…it's just…"

"I know. Come on now, I won't say a word if you flood me out. You deserve a good cry."

She flew into his arms. Nate hugged her close, holding her tight. Allie wrapped her arms around his waist, buried her head in his shirtfront and the tears came.

"Poor baby. Battle ignorance by day and klutzes by night. You're exhausted."

"I'm trying to be a good sport, I really am. And I feel so bad that I can't seem to…"

"I know, I know."

"It's just that, for the first time ever—" Allie stopped for a hiccup "—I had picked out everything by myself. I always wanted pink—my brothers teased me so badly about that and—it was just the way I wanted it." She hiccuped again, mortified by her loss of control and unable to do a darn thing about it. Her emotional dam had well and truly broken.

Nate felt about two inches tall. "Shh, you're going to make yourself sick, sweetheart. Try to take a deep breath. Come on, now."

"And your dad…"

Nate rolled his eyes. His father. She need go no further. If Nate couldn't find him a wife soon, he was thinking about contacting the CIA. They could use him for search and destroy missions. He'd be a natural.

"He's so sweet."

"Yes he is."

"You can't get mad at him."

Actually, you could, but it only made you feel worse. The guy had the best of intentions, after all.

"He feels so badly about everything."

Which did absolutely no good when you were left standing in the resulting rubble, but whatever. "I understand."

"It's just that—it's just that—shoot, I need a tissue."

"Allie, look at me." Nate understood her frustration. Man, did he understand. Maybe now was the time to try and recruit Allie to Project Wife Hunt. He tipped up her chin with two fingers. "Come on, look at me, sweetheart." Her eyes glistened with moisture, making them appear almost an emerald-green. Nate carefully swiped away the rivulets of tears with his fingers. "I have this idea—damn but you're pretty."

"I look awful when I cry. My eyes are all red and puffy, aren't they?"

"No, no, they're gorgeous. You're gorgeous."

"Phht. Get out. They're red. I know they're red."

"Okay, maybe they're a bit pink, but just a bit."

"I knew it!"

"But mostly they look like emeralds caught in a streambed." Nate felt compelled to congratulate himself. For a guy who had a tough time with dumb romantic stuff, that wasn't half bad. Best of all, it was true, which was maybe why it had come so easily. Her eyes really did look like liquid gemstones. And the tears shimmering in the thick dark lashes framing her eyes added to the general effect. Not that her crying was a good thing. It wasn't. But on Allie it looked good. "Allie?"

"What?"

"I think I need to kiss you."

Allie leaned back to get a better look at Nate's face. "Excuse me?"

Nate nodded decisively. "Yes, I really think I need to kiss you now."

"Nate?"

He leaned down and gently touched his lips to hers. "Hmm?"

"I—what—you—" Nate had readjusted his arms, snugging Allie in closer. His lips returned to begin nibbling on hers and darned if she could put a coherent thought together. She sighed instead.

"So good," Nate murmured against her lips. "So sweet. You sneaked a candy bar on the way home from school, didn't you, sweetheart?"

"Um, Butterfingers. The kids are selling them for a moneymaker."

"Uh-huh. Thought so." Nate widened the stance of his feet for better balance. "Can you part your lips a little bit, sugar? I'm thinking it's gonna be all honey inside there."

Stunned, Allie whispered, "Honey?"

"Thank you," Nate said, and slipped his tongue inside. Unwilling to scare her, Nate made an effort to be gentle. He lightly explored her teeth with only the tip of his tongue first. She moaned a little so Nate was pretty sure she liked it. He got bolder and slid his tongue past her teeth to play with hers, enticing it to respond and maybe return the favor. Allie's arms migrated northward until they were wrapped around his neck. Nate considered that a good sign. Then, when he withdrew his tongue from her mouth, sure enough, Allie's followed. There was no lingering doubt in Nate's mind. Allie was equally involved.

He ran his hands up and down her spine, then planted one firmly on her posterior locking her hips up against his. Nate tangled the remaining hand in her short auburn curls, holding her head in place while they basically ate each other alive.

"Man," Nate said, finally coming up for air. "You are lethal. How old did you say you were?"

Looking confused, Allie murmured, "Twenty-eight."

She cleared her throat as her head cleared a bit. "I'm twenty-eight. What of it?"

"I'm amazed somebody didn't scoop you up a long time ago, that's all," Nate confessed. "I mean, you go beyond hot. You're downright incendiary. How come you're still on the loose?"

Allie almost laughed, except it really wasn't funny. In all her twenty-eight years, no other guy had *ever* accused her of being even lukewarm let alone hot. Certainly not incendiary. Not her.

Nate blew out a breath. "Is there smoke coming out of my ears?"

Allie made a pretext of checking. "Nope. You're in the clear. Although I have to say it would be sort of interesting to have a guy spontaneously combust. Very ego building, you know?"

"I bet," Nate growled. Some guy? Some generic guy? He didn't think so. If anybody was going to spontaneously combust around Allison MacLord, it was going to darn well be Nathaniel Parker. Much as he hated giving his father any kind of victory in the war they currently fought, what the old man didn't know about couldn't really count, now could it?

The mood was broken. Thinking about his father did that to him, and Allie was caught up imagining Nate—or any guy for that matter, going up in smoke after kissing her. Yeah, right.

"I'm hungry," she said even though she wasn't, not really. The paint job by Jackson Pollock's replacement had pretty much taken away any appetite. The mention of food, however, usually worked to distract her brothers, and Allie thought a distraction was exactly what was needed right then. "How about you?"

Nate released his hold on her and rubbed the nape of his

neck. "Yeah, I could use something." He'd need his strength to deal with this latest disaster he supposed. "What are you in the mood for?"

"Uh…"

"Chinese? Mexican? Mickey D's?"

"Sure."

"Sure?" Nate laughed. "You *are* hungry."

No, she wasn't. What she was was acting like an idiot. Good Lord. Men had kissed her before. They'd never self-combusted and neither had Allie, but the act was not totally alien to her, either. *Get a grip,* she told herself. *The man's going to think you're more than a few French fries short of a Happy Meal.* "I don't really feel like going out," Allie confided. "Why don't we both raid our cupboards and see what we can come up with?"

A woman who preferred to stay in? Allie wasn't going to take advantage of the fact he was willing to spend money on her? Nate looked at her uncertainly, trying to read her mind. "You sure?"

Allie had already started for her kitchen. She glanced back over her shoulder. "Hmm? Oh, yes. I'm sure."

Weird. Mentally Nate shrugged. "I've got some hamburger meat in my fridge, I think."

"And I've got a can of kidney beans," said Allie, backing out of a cabinet with a can in hand. They looked at each other.

"Chili?"

"Sounds perfect. Bring your can and let's go upstairs. You got any chili powder? I think I'm out."

"Right here."

"Awesome. We're out of here." Nate slung his arm over Allie's shoulders and pulled her in close as they headed out of the door. He kept her right there for the elevator ride and didn't let go until he had to dig into his pockets for his key. He tried to tell himself it was to prevent a misstep and tumble down the steps, but the truth was Allie felt good there. It felt right, God help him.

"Just sit here," Nate said as he directed Allie into a kitchen chair. "As soon as I get out of this suit, we'll get dinner going. Won't take me but a couple of minutes."

"I can start…"

"No. You've had a bad day and the first time some hot woman cooks food for me in my own kitchen, well, I've got certain expectations that, trust me, you don't want to hear about."

Allie looked at him oddly. "What are you talking about? Expectations?"

Nate gave her a lopsided grin. "I shouldn't admit this out loud since you'll probably hit me, but I'm prone to all the typical male fantasies. I could really get into the mental image of the little woman wearing something slinky in the kitchen fixing my meals, especially after meeting me at the door with a drink." Nate sighed. "I know, I know, totally un PC. But it's a really great fantasy. From the male perspective. Maybe, if I ever decide to lose all personal freedom and actually get married, it could be sort of a perk." He brightened up. "Yeah, my wife might do it like, for a birthday or anniversary present. What do you think?" he asked, sounding hopeful.

Allie crossed her arms over his chest and glared. "And I suppose *the little woman* is dressed in something sick like clear plastic wrap, am I right?" She had brothers. She knew. "Men are so pathetic. Well, all I can say is it won't be me. Should I ever go temporarily out of my mind and think I was wildly in love or something, I might get talked into dinner, but I don't dress in plastic wrap for anybody."

Nate pretended to give it some thought. "No, I suppose you're not the plastic wrap type. Too obvious. You'd never be that blatant. Would you consider an apron? You know, if it was a special occasion like your husband's birthday? A significant one,'' he persisted when Allie still looked doubtful. Nate didn't know why he was pursuing this. The mental image was going to kill him. He'd be hard for a month at this rate. "Like the big three-oh." Why couldn't he let it go? The mental image just kept getting clearer and clearer. He'd be panting in a minute. "An apron's not asking so much, is it?''

"An apron?" Allie quizzed, puzzled. She'd been raised with all brothers and Allie would still never understand the male mind. Aprons were stupid looking. June Cleaver wore an apron, for heaven's sake. They were frilly and silly and…dumb.

"Yeah."

"Nobody uses an apron anymore. At least nobody I know. And what's sexy about an apron?''

"Oh, did I forget to mention that's all you'd be wearing?'' Oh, man, his brain was sizzling now with that picture.

Allie's mouth dropped open. "And I suppose it would be one of those ruffled ones straight out of the fifties?''

"I like the way you think. And see-through. No, translucent. You know, subtle but not opaque. A hint of what's underneath is way more sexy than a blatant display to my way of thinking. How about it?''

"In your dreams, buddy."

Nodding his head fervently, Nate agreed. "Yeah. And it gets better every time.''

"Nate Parker!''

"Hey, I'm a guy. I'm not responsible for my fantasies. They come with the androgen and testosterone. It's not like I plan on acting on it, although hope springs eternal. And don't tell me women don't fantasize.''

Allie wasn't about to admit to any such thing. "Well, maybe a little bit...but not like that!" And that was the truth. She'd never dreamed about a woman in a see-through apron meeting her at the door with a drink in hand. Not once.

"I don't think it qualifies as a fantasy unless the opposite sex is at least partially naked," Nate pointed out. "So, in your fantasy, what was the guy wearing?"

Allie threw up her hands. "Oh for heav—go change your clothes, will you?"

Grinning wickedly, Nate snapped off a salute. "Yes, ma'am."

Nate hung up his suit and grabbed a pair of jeans. He threw his tie over the back of a chair, unbuttoned the top few buttons of his oxford cloth shirt and rolled up the sleeves. Losing his dress shoes, he padded into the bathroom in his socks.

Teasing Allie was fun, Nate thought to himself as he used cool water on his face in an attempt to rinse away the day's tiredness. To tell the truth, bantering with Allie had been amazingly reinvigorating all by itself. He and Jared were putting in so many hours trying to get the business up and running, Nate was usually too tired to go out in the evenings. His dinners were mostly out of a can and solitary, eaten standing up at the countertop, which eliminated the need for clearing his briefcase and papers off the kitchen table. Nate strove for honesty, and he would be the first one to admit he had a tendency to fall into a routine. Sue him, he liked the predictability of it. But tonight was going to be different and Nate found himself eager to get back out to the kitchen so he could cook dinner with Allie.

He gave his face a cursory glance in the mirror, decided shaving would be too obvious. He didn't want Allie thinking he was trying to impress her or anything. And besides,

Nate thought as he ran a hand over his chin and felt the
light sandpaper effect, his five-o'clock shadow looked kind
of studly. Some women liked a little bit of bristle. There
was always the possibility Allie might be one. Not that he
intended to give her preferences a second thought. Nate
turned his chin, checked that view. "Yes, definitely
studly." He had to laugh at himself then, shook his head
at his own ridiculousness and left the bathroom still chuck-
ling and almost mowed Allie down.

"Oops!"

Nate reached out a hand to steady her. "Allie! I'm sorry!
What are you doing in here?"

Allie transferred the drink she held to the opposite hand
and licked her fingers where it had sloshed over. "I brought
you a drink," she said, and shrugged. "My little attempt
at humor. I thought you'd think it was funny."

Nate took the proffered drink and waggled his eyebrows.
"But where's the apron? That was going to be the best
part."

Allie snorted. "Take the drink and be grateful."

He sighed and sipped. "It's apple juice," Nate said
blankly.

"That was all I could find."

"There is a bottle of wine out there somewhere. I'll look
for it."

"Okay. Just get a move on. I'm starving." And suddenly
she was. It was no hardship to spend the evening with
Nate—provided she didn't think about the condition of her
apartment. The faded jeans he'd changed into hugged his
lean hips. They'd been zipped but not buttoned and there
was something incredibly sexy about watching him do up
that top button, which only proved she was losing her grip.
Hadn't she watched her brothers do up their snaps plenty
of times? Heck, Allie had even *helped* the younger ones.

The T-shirt Nate had pulled over his head was old and had obviously shrunk from its many washings. It was snug enough now that she could see the muscles of his chest ripple underneath the thinned cotton and there was a very sexy hole starting in the fabric down by his belly button. He was shoeless—why shouldn't a man be comfortable in his own home? He didn't *need* a shave, it's not like he was going to work or anything, but the bit of stubble he sported and his tousled hair gave him a slightly disreputable air.

If she hadn't noticed it before, Allie was noticing it now. Nate Parker was *hot!*

Unfortunately for her, Allie knew her limitations. She could notice all she wanted, but the fact remained that while Nate might tease her, there was not a doubt in her mind that she was in no danger. Allie had a lot of guy friends, but they treated her more like a sister than anyone who might inspire lust. Not that she *wanted* to be hassled or anything, still it would be nice to know that somebody at least thought of her that way. Well, another woman would understand. And it didn't matter anyway, because if there was one thing Allie knew, it was that she was safe with Nate. Heck, she'd practically slept on top of the poor man and he'd been a perfect gentleman.

Except, there had been that kiss.

Darn, but she was confused.

Nate smiled at her. Oh, man, why did he have to do that? It only confused her more.

"Let's go get the chili started."

"Right. Food. We'll eat." Maybe she was becoming hypoglycemic and her blood sugar was off. That could explain why she felt funny. Blood sugar problems affected your brain and your thought processes. Of course! That had to be it. She wasn't losing it, thank God. She just hadn't been terribly hungry at lunchtime and even the little she'd eaten

then had been used up hours ago. Allie approved of logic
and things that made sense. The convoluted thinking that
went along with things of the heart only confused her, and
Allie told herself to forget about them. She'd eat instead.
Eating would make everything better. Right.

Out in the kitchen, Allie unwrapped the ground beef
while Nate dug out a frying pan. She broke up the beef in
the skillet with a spoon while Nate diced an onion. She
measured chili powder while Nate opened the can of kidney
beans. She added cumin, paprika and oregano. Nate opened
a can of diced tomatoes and one of tomato paste. In under
fifteen minutes, chili bubbled on the stove top. Its fragrant
aroma filled the room, teasing their noses and making them
both crowd the stove, eyeing the pot hungrily.

"How long do you think it needs to simmer to blend the
flavors?" Allie asked.

"The flavors need to blend?"

"Well, yes."

"Oh." Nate scratched his chin and watched the skillet
while he considered that. "How long do you usually let it
simmer when you make it?" He'd just been getting into
cooking when he and Jared had started the business. Work
took most of his energy at this point in time. His chili was
out of a can now. The hamburger in his refrigerator had
originally been purchased to add to a box of Hamburger
Helper.

"All afternoon."

That broke him out of his reverie. His attention switched
to Allie. "All afternoon? No way." He made an executive
decision right then and there. "It's got however long it
takes us to get the bowls out and crunch up some corn
chips to put on top. That's it. Then we eat."

Allie shrugged. "Okay." She was more than willing to
eat the chili a bit early. Because now that there was nothing

to do but watch the pot, Allie was becoming very aware of Nate, the man again, as she stood beside him in his small kitchen. He was tall, like her brothers. She only came up to Nate's chin. He was broad shouldered, again like her brothers. Allie would be willing to bet he lifted. Two of her brothers even had blue eyes like Nate.

So how come he felt so totally unbrotherish to her?

Allie flushed and hoped Nate couldn't read minds. So he'd teased her a little. Her brothers could be downright merciless, and she knew better than to read anything into a little teasing.

It was definitely time for another distraction before she got all tangled up in her own thought processes. Personally she was beginning to doubt that what was passing through her mind of late qualified for that definition. Whatever. Allie cleared her throat. "Where are the bowls?" she asked.

"Up there." Nate pointed. No way was Nate going to wait any longer for the meat to soak up flavor. The scent of chili was strong in the room, but it was Allie's essence that filled all his senses. They either ate now or he took her on the kitchen table, one or the other.

Feeling a little bit desperate, Nate reached for the bag of Fritos he'd stored in an upper cabinet. He set it on the counter and smashed it a couple of times with his fist. It took a lot to push Nate to violence, but being confined in close quarters with Allie over the past two days had the real possibility of pushing him right over the edge. "Check the fridge, will you? See if there's any cheese?"

Allie watched his fist come down one more time on the hapless bag of chips. One brow rose. "Uh, sure. You know, you might want to take it easy there. I think you're reducing them to crumbs."

"What?" Nate scowled at the bag. "Oh, right. Wouldn't

want crumbs. I guess I was kind of taking my frustrations out on them, wasn't I?''

Nate growled. He was irritated with himself for the way he'd flirted and teased with her earlier. Talk about playing into his father's hand. ''Quit being so damn understanding, will you? I feel bad enough as it is without you being so stinking *nice* about everything.''

From the way he sneered the word *nice,* Allie guessed it wasn't a compliment. She retrieved an open bag of shredded cheddar from the refrigerator and held it up to the light. Nothing blue or fuzzy that she could see. ''Yes, it would really help the situation if I yelled and screamed. I can see how you'd prefer that.''

''At least if you were being witchy about it I wouldn't feel so low.''

''Sorry to disappoint you, but I gave up broom flying when the engine on my broom threw a rod. Never have gotten around to replacing it.'' Allie brushed her hair out of her face. ''Can we eat now?''

Nate scrubbed a hand over his face. ''Man. Yeah, sorry. None of this is your fault.''

Allie smirked. ''True. It's yours. There. Does that make you feel better? How about this?'' Allie struck a dramatic pose. ''You've ruined my life.''

''Me?'' Nate bobbled his bowl. ''I had nothing to do with any of this! My father—''

''If you didn't live here, your father would not have been under this sink playing with the garbage disposal, now would he?''

Nate dumped a double fistful of grated cheddar and Frito crumbs on top of his chili. ''Now just a cotton-picking sec—''

Allie daintily ladled the spiced ground beef into her bowl. ''Would he?''

"Well, technically, no, I guess not but—"

"See, told you so. It is too all your fault." She sat at the table and stuck her spoon in the bowl. "There. Now you should be downright ecstatic. Everything's your fault."

Well, damn, this wasn't quite what he'd had in mind, either.

Nate plunked himself down into a chair and jabbed at his chili with his spoon. When he pulled the utensil back out, strings of melting cheese with corn chip crumbs clung like cheap pearls stretched out. He cut them off with a swipe of his finger and scowled at Allie.

She smiled sweetly in return and shoveled in a bite. Immediately she fanned her mouth. "Ooh, hot! Hot! Quick, have you got any milk or water?"

Nate swiveled in his chair, opened the fridge and grabbed the milk container. Quickly he poured her a glass. "Here. Drink this to put out the fire then I'll try to find the wine. You know, if you weren't so busy baiting me, you probably wouldn't have burned your mouth. You need to be more careful. You—"

Allie made a face. "Oh, hush." She gestured to his bowl. "Eat your food. It's hot, but it's awesome tasting. We're a good team." She took another, more careful, spoonful. "Mmm. We done good, Nate. This tastes fine. Eat up."

Nate considered her thoughtfully. He tried the chili. They did make a good team. It was fine. His dad, strictly by accident, of course, could have picked a winner.

Nate really hated that.

Chapter Eight

After dinner Nate planted himself on the sofa, picked up the remote control and found himself a baseball game. Allie remained at the table grading papers.

The game was long and boring without much action. Nate did a little channel surfing.

India. Allie read on the paper she graded. *The state next to ours.* She shook her head, used her red pen to make a check mark. Indiana was next to Illinois, not India, Einstein. Next time study a bit. "Nate?"

"Hmm?"

"Could you do me a huge favor?"

"Sure. What do you need?"

"Could you pick a station, any station, and leave it there? You're changing channels so fast I don't see how you can even tell what's on them. It's really distracting."

"It's a guy thing," Nate informed her, surprised Allie wasn't already aware of that particular male idiosyncrasy. Surely she hadn't lived twenty-eight years under a cabbage leaf. Some things were just basic knowledge after all.

"Yes, I know. My father and brothers do it all the time. It's annoying. I can't concentrate and I need to. I've got some kid who thinks India is part of the United States."

Nate snorted. "You mean it isn't?"

"Ha-ha."

Restless, Nate hit the power button and tossed the remote onto the couch. He rose and wandered over to the table. "What are you doing?"

"Correcting papers. Then I need to do some lesson plans."

He reached for the stack in front of Allie. "Here. I'll do this. You get to your planning."

"You don't have to—"

"Just give them to me, okay? I can do this for you. I want to. Uh, you've got an answer key, right?"

Allie rolled her eyes. "Here. This kid got them all right. Use hers."

"Okay."

They worked quietly for a few minutes. Nate got up and put some classical radio station on in the background. He returned to his spot. "Do people who live in India have six arms?" he read out loud. "That would make a good research paper? Why would a topic like that even occur to someone? What have you been teaching these kids?" he questioned Allie.

"We were talking about India and its culture. Shiva, one of the three main gods of Hinduism is portrayed with six arms. He's in charge of a bunch of stuff. Guy's got a lot to do. Evidently he needs them. Marcus must have extrapolated from there. Write 'see me' across that suggestion and skip the rest of the research topic ideas on the other papers. I'll take care of that part."

"I've got a handle on it. Just surprised me is all." Nate followed Allie's directive, writing *"see me"* in red. After a moment of thought, he added, *"You may have difficulty finding resources for your topic."* Two arms were kind of a given. There probably wasn't much research devoted to the possibility of six. "Allie?"

"Hmm?"

"What's your favorite fantasy?"

Allie looked up from her lesson plan book. "What?"

"You know, your favorite fantasy. I told you mine. I was just...wondering about yours."

"I want to win the lottery. But only if it's at least thirty or forty million that week. Anything less isn't worth it. And it needs to be fast. A couple of my brothers need new cars and my dad's making noises about wanting to build a retirement place. Oh, and the school where I work needs new computers."

"This kid here says Shiva likes to stand on a dwarf? That one of his arms is supposed to look like an elephant trunk? You've got a drug problem in this school?"

"I showed them a picture of a statue in the Art Institute. The kid's right. He's also got a little praying dude stuck in his hair and has flames coming out of one palm."

"Cool."

"My students thought so."

"Allie, I'm serious. You said you had a fantasy about your dream man. What was it?"

"It's stupid."

Nate's brow rose. "Dumber than the transparent apron?"

"Nothing's dumber than the transparent apron."

"Well then?"

Allie sighed, and raked a hand through her hair. "All right, all right. Fair's fair. Here goes. You know how your perfect woman is a fluff-brained moron who doesn't mind waiting on you and likes parading around mostly naked?"

Nate had to smile. "Yeah, that would be great. I mean, so?"

"Well, I'm a pretty good athlete. Growing up with nothing but boys in the house, I guess you could say I was kind of a tomboy. As the only girl, I wouldn't give an inch and I excelled out of necessity. But there's a problem with being better than a guy at sports. They whine when they lose, and I don't throw any contest just to soothe some lamebrain's ego."

And here Nate had thought women were out looking for guys who were in touch with their feminine side. Nate barely bit back a snort. As if. Well, now he didn't have to get all depressed over the fact he didn't have one. Maybe there was hope.

"It's not that I don't know I'm being contrary since I take great delight in beating my brothers' butts wherever and whenever possible. I can pretty much outdo them at whatever, but every now and then, in one of my weaker moments I think about dating a man who can, say, out hit me when we go to the batting cages."

"You want to get it on with a baseball player?" Well, he'd heard some guys considered guns to be an extension of their manhood. What about baseball bats? Did they count? Yikes, what a thought.

"I know, I know, it's stupid. But I'd settle for one who at least doesn't whine when I kick his rear in a game of horse."

She wanted to play horse? Nate would go along with the gag provided he got to play the stallion. Oh, wait, she meant with a basketball. Nuts. "That's it? Your fantasy evening with a guy is playing sports?" Weird chick. Although it could be a guy's dream date. How many women liked sports, after all? He didn't have any sisters, so it was hard to know, but the ladies he'd dated would have whined

big time had he suggested a date involving a basketball
hoop. He'd have to think about this. No, a key element was
missing here. And Nate knew just what it was.

Nate placed a red check mark on the paper in front of
him. The Mississippi was not a river considered sacred in
India last time he checked. "What kind of fantasy is it if
nobody gets naked?" Nate complained. "Come on, somebody's got to be at least partially naked."

"Get off the nakedness thing, will you?" Allie said,
"You know how guys can't talk about feelings and emo-
tions?"

The mere idea made him queasy. "Yeah?"

"My fantasy man is all man, you know, a little bit macho, wildly in love with me and totally able to not only
admit it, but talk about his feelings for me."

Sick. That was just plain sick. "You couldn't settle for
being naked?" Wasn't that just like a woman? Nate rolled
his eyes. They had to *talk*. And not just any topic would
do. It had to be about *feelings*. He got nauseous just thinking about it. Here's what Nate wanted to know. How come
men had the more defined, larger jaws? It was women who
exercised theirs half to death with all their *meaningful di-
alogue* stupid stuff.

Allie simply did not understand why men were so fixated
on women losing their clothing. Didn't they get that a little
communication, some—God forbid—*conversation* would
get them a lot further than jumping the poor woman's bones
right off the bat? "No." She was adamant. "I couldn't
settle for that." It may be a fantasy, but it was *her* fantasy
and *her* guy would be crazy about her and have no problems owning up to it. And they'd both have on clothes.
There was always the possibility they'd lose them later as
the fantasy developed, but they'd at least start off with
them on.

Nate scowled. Well, damn. "Maybe he could beat up somebody for you," he suggested. "An evil troll?" Why he cared, since he had no intention of starring in Allie's fantasy, Nate couldn't really say.

Allie's nose scrunched up at the idea, although she'd met a few troll-like men in her time who could have used a good whomping.

"Go on a quest," Nate continued hopefully. "You know, *do* something." Anything but talk about feelings. That was just so not a guy thing to do. How the woman could say she wanted a macho man and then with the very next breath say he had to be able to *express* himself on a level meaningful to a *woman*—it was ridiculous, was what. One of her requirements excluded the other and the whole concept made Nate squirm.

"What's the matter?"

"Nothing." Nate forced himself to remove the look of distaste from his face. "How about if he fought a dragon for you?"

"No such thing."

"It's a fantasy," he quickly pointed out. "There could be a dragon if you wanted."

Allie scrunched her nose again while she considered that. Darn, she was cute when she did that. Made him want to kiss it all smooth again.

"Well, maybe. I could dress him up in a medieval outfit. My guy will have well-defined calves and thighs since he's all athletic so he'd look good in tights, you know?"

Tights? Good God. He'd rather talk about feelings.

"And he could maybe wear my favor of a scarf or something while he fought a dragon for me although I can't see why it's so important to you. It's *my* fantasy, after all. I let you have yours and I didn't criticize."

"Yes, you did," Nate quickly pointed out. He had absolutely no idea why he wanted to rewrite Allie's fantasy either. It certainly wasn't so he could attempt to fulfill it for her, that was for sure.

"Okay, maybe I laughed a little bit. But, I still don't want anybody naked…or even partially naked in my fantasy."

"All right, all right, no nudity. Tough to fight a dragon in the buff anyway. Good way to get burned."

"You're right. I didn't think of that. Good point."

"Yeah, yeah, fine, they'll wear clothes." The wearing-clothes thing had Nate losing interest. "Let's go to bed."

"Excuse me?" Allie's eyebrows rose and there was an arch tone to her voice.

Nate shoved the stack of papers aside. "I'm through with these…your kids are clueless, by the way…at least when it comes to India. It's getting late, I'm tired, you're yawning, so let's go to bed."

"So what you're saying here is, let's go to sleep, right?"

"I'm too tired to argue semantics with you." Nate rose from his chair.

"No, wait. Let's talk about this."

Oh, God, here they went again. If his eyes rolled any farther around, he'd be looking out the back of his head. "No. We're not going to have a meaningful conversation about this. That's ridiculous. I'm tired, you're tired, we'll brush our teeth, go prone, cover up, close our eyes and voilá, REM, uh, rapid eye movement takes over. In other words, sleep. That's it. No *talking* necessary."

"So we're talking sleeping, as in snoring, right?"

"What else? You won't even consider nakedness even in a fantasy. Now come on, up with you. Get ready for bed. And I don't snore."

Allie had risen, but she stalled out again with the mention

of the word *bed.* "I'll take the sofa tonight. You can have the bed."

"We already know that doesn't work. It's a king-size bed. I won't touch you."

That wasn't what she was worried about, Allie thought gloomily. It hadn't been Nate crossing the invisible midline of the bed last night. How was she to control what she did in her sleep? And what if she did it again tonight? Nate would think she was wanton. Or hard up. Either one was unacceptable to Allie's way of thinking. And it was all so unfair, anyway. It was hardly her fault the man radiated heat like a furnace. She'd never been so warm. Frankly, in Allie's estimation, Nate could make a fortune renting out his body on cold winter nights. A hot-water bottle or an electric blanket just wasn't the same thing.

"Really, I—"

Nate tugged to get her moving. "Shh. I said no talking, meaningful or otherwise."

Allie put her free hand on her hip. "I'm perfectly capable of making my own deci—"

"I said to hush. I'm being macho. Enjoy it. And if you can't enjoy it, deal with it. We're adults. We can both be comfortable without jumping each other." Although from Nate's perspective, it was going to be difficult. Allie was seriously cute and the better he got to know her, the cuter she got. He was actually kind of hopeful last night would repeat itself. Allie could hardly accuse him of taking advantage when she was the one who came to him, now could she? Nate intended to sleep with one eye open tonight. That way, if Allie decided to snuggle he'd be aware enough to enjoy it. "Now hop to it."

Well, really, Allie humphed to herself. Tugging did nothing to free herself. She was being literally, inexorably, for all its gentleness, *hauled* to the bathroom. All right, maybe

if she repeated *stay on your own side* over and over, kind
of like a mantra, so it was her last thought before she fell
asleep—maybe that would work. It was worth a try since
Nate was obviously incapable of listening to reason.

Furthermore, she was going to have to seriously revamp
her fantasy life. Allie was rapidly coming to the conclusion
that macho men were a giant pain. They didn't listen worth
a darn.

Allie let Nate maneuver her into the bathroom. She
loaded up her toothbrush and set to work shining her smile.
Her parents had paid a fortune for that smile and Allie
wondered how badly it would slip if she went another night
without her retainers. She was supposed to wear them once
or twice a week to prevent her teeth from shifting back.
She really should…

"Oh, pht. I'm not wearing them tonight. They make me
lisp."

Maybe she could sneak them into the nightstand drawer.
Then, once she was sure Nate was sound asleep, she
could…

"No."

Allie rinsed her mouth and checked her smile out in the
mirror. Was her one front tooth turning and protruding just
the smallest bit?

"Yes." Allie sighed. She'd better stick them in.

But say she happened to roll over onto Nate's side of
the bed again. Totally without her own knowledge, of
course. Say that was to happen and she ended up in Nate's
arms again.

"It could happen," Allie told herself as she ran her
tongue along the slight protuberance. A person couldn't be
responsible for what they did when they were asleep, after
all.

And then, say Nate was to try and oh, *kiss* her, for example. Say he was to *French* kiss her. Wouldn't he feel the retainers with his tongue?

"Yes." She'd leave them off.

Allie felt the little bump one more time with the tip of her tongue and rolled her eyes. "This is ridiculous." She was becoming a blathering idiot. Rinsing her retainers in the tap water, she shoved them in and left the bathroom feeling all defiant and ready for a confrontation.

"Let him try and say something," she mumbled to herself. "He objects to a little bit of plastic in my mouth? Well, who cares what Mr. Naturally Perfect Teeth thinks? If that's the biggest problem to crop up in his life, he's got it made in the shade, doesn't he? I mean, talk about shallow! If he thinks for one minute that I—"

Allie was still quietly ranting as she rounded the corner into the bedroom. There she came to a dead halt. The object of her rant was propped up in bed, glasses propped on the bridge of his nose, quietly reading a book. While Allie had been stewing and worrying over his reaction to some orthodontia, Nate had been totally relaxed, not concerned at all with what *she'd* think about his less than perfect eyesight.

Nate glanced up from the book he'd been engrossed in and took in her heightened coloring. "What's up?"

"Nothing." Allie gestured futilely. "I, uh, didn't know you wore glasses."

"Usually I wear contacts." Without one or the other, one of his eyes tended to develop a mind of its own and go off course. Not that he was about to share that little tidbit. They were working together for the moment.

"Uh-huh." She nodded her head. Darn, he looked cute in them. The frames were thin, black and designed to compliment the shape of his face. The lenses made his blue eyes appear even larger and she was one dead duck.

Allie clenched her fists. This was so unfair! She was
stuck with a mouthful of plastic while Nate's compensation
for his minor flaw made him look even better.

Nate's head was cocked. "You sound different," he said.
"You chewing on something? I thought you brushed your
teeth."

Allie sighed. So much for sneaking one over on him.
"Retainers," she said, grimacing when the *s* came out more
like a *th*. "It's been a while, so I really need to wear them
tonight."

"Are they that new space-age material with shape memory?" Nate asked.

Allie's brows rose. "Yes. They are."

"Cool," he said, and patted the bed next to him in a
gesture meant as an invitation to join him. He stuck his
nose back in his book. "Just getting good," Nate said, by
way of explanation.

That was it? Allie stood staring at him, briefly frozen.
The expression *left with your mouth hanging open* came
vividly alive in her mind. It took real concentration to keep
her jaw locked in place. That was *it?* She'd agonized in the
bathroom all that time and all he had to say was they were
cool because they had shape memory capabilities? Well,
maybe she should just flip them out and hand them to him.
Let Nate examine them up close. Oh, no, wait, he was too
involved in his reading to bother with anything having to
do with her. The book was just getting good, after all.

What a clod.

What a jerk.

Allie squinted and examined the cover. Okay, so it was
a John Grisham and he was pretty good. Allie was forced
to acknowledge that much, being basically the honest type.
But nope, Grisham or not, the excuse still didn't cut it in
her book. Allie didn't care if it was William Shakespeare,

when a woman climbed into bed with you, you could at least sit up and take notice.

Allie pulled the sheet and blanket back, got into bed, positioned herself so close to the edge that she should probably hang on to prevent falling out, and presented Nate with her back.

And furthermore, Allie decided, after she'd settled herself, it didn't matter that she wasn't wearing something slinky. So she wasn't the obvious type. Sue her.

He was still a clod.

On the opposite side of the bed, Nate struggled to remember what he'd just read, with little luck. He sighed and went back to the top of the page. Again. If Grisham couldn't hold him, nothing could. He was in serious trouble. Nate doubted he was going to make it through the night without doing something stupid.

There was a murder going on right beneath his nose. Murder! And all Nate could pay attention to was Allie's unique perfume, which wasn't really perfume at all, just her own special blend of soap, clean hair and woman. It was very subtle, like the sweet curves of Allie's body. You almost had to concentrate to ignore it because it worked more on your subconscious, he guessed. Sort of like those pheromone things he'd read about when he'd been desperate for reading material in the dentist's waiting room last time. Before you even realized it and could get your defenses up into place, you were all hot and bothered and panting like a long-haired dog who'd been chasing his own tail on a hot summer day.

As a matter of fact, Nate *did* sort of feel as if he'd been running around in circles since Allie had come on the scene. Didn't it kind of seem like cheating for a woman to work on your subconscious like that when—

Damn! Here he was at the bottom of the page again with no idea how the guy'd been done in.

Nate gave up. He closed the book and tossed it onto the nightstand, flicked off the light and grimly slid down under the blanket and sheet. He turned on his side and gave Allie *his* back. Damn woman with her stupid pheromones.

Ten minutes later he tried his stomach.

After twenty minutes he was flat on his back.

At the half-hour mark, he reluctantly rolled onto his left side, which Nate already knew would be a mistake. Now he was facing Allie in a position where, with his eyes adjusted to the dark now, he could tell that she and her restless movements had the air in the room all churned up. Her special fragrance kept wafting over his face. It was killing him. Never mind the guy in Grisham's book. Nate was the one dying.

Come on, Allie, roll over this way.

Maybe if he willed it strongly enough, kind of like the way Yoda taught Luke Skywalker, he could make it happen. Once Nate had Allie in his arms, he doubted he'd be able to sleep, but heck, he wasn't sleeping now, either, now was he? And if Nate was holding her, at least the itch in his hands that had him desperate to reach for her would let up.

"Nate?"

Never would he admit to startling. "Yeah?"

"You asleep?"

God, he wished. "What do you think?" Oh, good, snap her head off. That'll have her working her way over to your side of the bed real soon. Idiot.

"Sorry," Allie whispered.

Nate sighed and flopped onto his back. He stacked his hands behind his head. "It's okay. What did you want?"

"I can't sleep."

"Yeah. Me neither."

"But I'm so tired."

"Me, too."

"What should we do?"

Nate could think of any number of helpful suggestions, most of which would probably get his face slapped. Or worse. "I don't know."

"Maybe we should go for a walk."

"I'm not getting dressed again. We just got undressed."

"Yeah." She thought about that for a moment. "It's dark out," she offered tentatively. "Maybe nobody would notice what we were wearing."

"No. It's not only dark, it's late. We'd probably get mugged." He could almost hear her chewing on her lip. All Nate could think about was soothing it with his tongue.

"Okay, okay, no need to get your blood pressure up. Uh, watch a movie?"

"There's nothing on. I checked. Cubs don't play until Saturday, the Bears are off and none of the movie channels have anything decent, either."

"Oh. Do you want to talk?"

Nate almost exploded right then and there. Women! Of all the…no, he didn't want to talk. If Allie wasn't careful, Nate was going to take great pleasure in informing her exactly what he did want to do. Nate wanted to kiss her. Make that kiss her all over her body. He wanted to pull that oversize T-shirt up, lower her sweatpants and plant his lips on her belly. Exploring Allie's navel with his tongue sounded good, too. Nuzzling under and between her breasts ranked right up there, and tasting what he was sure would be tight little dusky-pink nipples, well, that was top of the list. Oh, but it would be ungentlemanly of him to forget her face, downright stupid to neglect her mouth. He sure hoped Allie spoke some French, 'cause that's how he was going to kiss her.

Nate gritted his teeth together. If he got any harder, he would risk going brittle. Then he'd be afraid to move for fear of bumping himself on something and having the proof of his masculinity shatter into a million itty-bitty pieces, which would pretty much kiss off the prospects of ever having children of his own. "Scoot over this way."

"What?"

"You look like you're going to fall off the bed. Scoot over. I don't bite." Much. "More. More."

"But…"

"There." Nate wrapped her up in his arms, cushioned her head on his chest. He was careful to angle his lower body away from her. "You slept just fine like this last night. Close your eyes. I'll rub your back for you until you drift off." One of them might as well get some rest. It sure as heck wasn't going to be him.

Man, if he got any more noble, he'd be up for knight-hood. If only he was English. Then again, Allie was at least part Scottish and Nate didn't think the English and Scots got along all that well, so maybe it was for the best. He ran his hands up and down her back. God, she felt good under his touch.

Allie snuggled into his chest. Nate smelled so…male. She burrowed her nose in, loving the way his crisp chest hair lightly abraded her cheek. Nate's smell was something appropriately manly. What? This time she actually rubbed her nose against him, too lost in identifying his scent to realize the dark offered no protection against Nate's *feeling* what she was doing. Irish Spring? Allie inhaled once more. Yes, she thought so. Yum!

Nate was more wide-awake than ever. What was the woman doing? Once he'd gotten Allie over here, she'd snuggled up like a kitten and if she didn't stop moving around she'd end up with a quick lesson in the extent of male self-control—or lack thereof. "Allie, baby, hold still," he all but begged, refused to whimper. What, did she think he was made of stone? Oops, bad analogy.

She suspected the bottoms he wore were a concession and she appreciated it, but she appreciated his bare chest more.

Allie froze. What was Nate growling about? He was the one who'd told her to scoot over by him. "Nate?"

"Yeah?" Her face was turned away from his chest and she was no longer nuzzling his chest. Thank you, God. He might survive the night yet.

"You're rubbing too hard on my back. It hurts."

"Oh, damn, baby, I'm sorry." He immediately lightened his touch to featherweight brushes. "Better?"

"Thanks. Am I too heavy? Am I hurting your shoulder?"

"Not at all. Now close your eyes and relax. Try to sleep." Nate couldn't help it. He kissed her forehead.

"Good night, Nate."

"Good night, sweetheart."

Wrapped in his arms, Allie drifted off almost immediately, caught up in a warm glow. Nate had called her sweetheart. Wasn't that...sweet? Nate, on the other hand, lay there staring at the ceiling for a long, long time before his own eyes closed.

Chapter Nine

"Ted, would you mind taking Tyrone, Lakeesha, Tiffany and Jarel into the hallway and quizzing them on their multiplication tables?"

Nate's father puffed out his chest. If he'd been wearing suspenders, Allie suspected he would have popped them. "No problem. Let's go, friends. Who's got the flash cards?"

"We don't have any," Allie explained. "We had to put the money into toner for the copier." She handed him a deck of playing cards she'd brought from home. "Just hold up the first two cards and have them multiply them. Jacks are eleven, queens twelve and I took out the kings since they don't have to know their thirteens by heart."

Ted took the deck. "Right."

"Mary Beth was wondering if you'd come down to third grade at eleven and work with a reading group."

"Sure."

"And Mike asked me to see if you'd be willing to work

on spelling with some kids he's got who are struggling. He thought maybe when you were done with Mary Beth."

Ted nodded. "Okay." He took a pad and pencil from his pocket and noted down the requests. "Anything else? I've got about forty minutes starting around one-thirty."

"Well, Mrs. Johnson…"

Ted perked right up. "The principal? Monica?"

"Yes, she was wondering if you could walk through the library with her, give her your input on rearranging and updating it."

"Monica wants my advice?" Ted sounded a little dazed.

"That's what she said."

"I'd be happy to. I'll stop by her office on my way to third grade and tell her one-thirty." And he carefully marked it down on his pad.

"Thanks, Ted. I can't tell you how great it is having you here. The teachers are all crazy about you."

"Really?"

Ted preened and Allie had to smile. Since his retirement, Allie suspected Ted was more used to groaning than gratitude when he was around. She was going to have to talk to Nate about that. "Really. They're all talking about what a huge help you are and what a difference you've made already."

"Well, you tell them it's my pleasure."

"I will, Ted, I will."

"All right, kids, out in the hall. Multiplication is important. You need to know this stuff. Just last week I was in the hardware store because I was going to do a little painting for Ms. MacLord here and I had to figure out…"

Ted guided the students out the door and Allie shook her head as he closed the door after himself. What a character. They had started week two of Ted's escort and tutorial service at the Academy of St. Stephen the Martyr. Thursday

and Friday of last week and Monday and Tuesday of this
week had been enough to give the overworked staff a small
taste of freedom. Planning periods were unheard-of luxuries
around St. Stephen's. Teachers taught all day every day.
They couldn't afford a lunchroom monitor so the teachers
even ate with the kids. At the end of the day, they took
turns helping with the after-school child-care program. Papers were corrected and planning taken care of after that.
The schedule was crazy, the pay low and the burnout rate
high.

Ted was a godsend and judging by the energy in his step
as he consulted the schedule in his notebook and hustled
from one classroom to another, he was enjoying the feeling
of being needed he sensed here.

As well he should, because he was.

When two-thirty rolled around and Allie had set her children free with admonitions to be careful on the way home,
she turned to Ted. "Wednesday's my day to stay late, Ted.
I can't leave at three-thirty like normal. It's going to be
closer to six. Why don't you go ahead and leave. I'll catch
a ride with one of the other teachers who's staying."

"I'll wait," Ted said. "No point making somebody else
go out of their way."

"Mary Beth won't mind. It's only half a mile extra for
her and you'll be bored."

"I'll wait," he insisted stubbornly. "And I won't be
bored. I always have a book with me but I doubt I'll get
to it. I've got some thinking and planning to do on those
changes Monica wants for the library."

"Okay," Allie said dubiously, "but if you change your
mind, just let me know. Mary Beth and I do this a lot for
each other when our cars need servicing or whatever."

He patted her hand. "Don't fret. Take care of whatever
you need to. I won't be bored."

And he wasn't. Ted wandered around the old outdated library for a while, letting ideas percolate, then stopped by the after-school child-care program. There, he ended up teaching some of the older children how to play chess. By six o'clock, he was bubbling over with plans for a chess tournament and finding someone to stencil chessboards directly on the old scarred wooden library tables.

"Have to strip them down and sand them real good before we can stencil or paint on them," he told her as he wove through the traffic on the Dan Ryan. He banged the steering wheel. "Look at that! Cut me right off! Idiot's lucky I didn't rear-end him. Where's a cop when you need one?"

Allie didn't know where the police were, probably avoiding the Ryan at this time of day if they were smart. A person could get killed the way people drove on Chicago's streets and highways, especially during the rush hours. She was also unsure who would have ended up with the ticket had there been a cop foolish enough to risk his life on the highway just then. Ted didn't exactly have all the rules of the road down by heart himself. He seemed to think the posted speed limits were suggestions rather than ticketable offenses should you choose to exceed them. Even though she was wearing her belt and shoulder strap, Allie braced a hand on the dashboard. "Uh, I've got some craft books at home. I'll bring them tomorrow—you are coming tomorrow, aren't you?"

Ted shot her a glance. "Of course."

"Okay, I didn't want to assume. I'll bring them and you can look through them. See if there are any suggestions for stenciling the tabletops you can use."

"Good idea. Maybe I'll stop by Borders or Barnes and Noble after I drop you off. See what they've got."

"You coming up for dinner?" Allie asked as he pulled up in front of her condo building.

"Not tonight. Too much to do. I'll find something at home or go through a drive-through."

"All right, if you're sure. I'll see you in the morning, then."

"Right. Six forty-five. I'll be here."

"Good night, Ted."

"Good night, Allie. Make sure that son of mine takes care of you."

"Not to worry, Ted. I can take care of myself."

"Even so."

Allie laughed. "Okay, okay. I'll make sure." Ted waited until she was in the foyer. She waved through the glass door as he drove off.

Allie was tired. Teaching in the inner city meant she had to be focused every second of the day, so she knew it was more mental than physical. Allie elected to take the stairs. Stopping into her own place, she sighed over the condition of the ceiling and changed her clothes. The good news was, the swelling in her door was down and she could at least lock the place up. The bad news was, in an attempt to air the musty smell out, Ted had suggested leaving the sliding doors to the small balcony patio off the living room open when he'd picked her up yesterday. Naturally it had rained even though rain had not been predicted and, naturally, the direction of the wind had driven said rain into the living room. Now *that* carpet was wet and starting to smell. The lady she'd borrowed the wet vac from was out of town which meant the wet vac was out of reach and Allie figured the door would be swollen again shortly. Ted had insisted on sprinkling baking soda to help with the odor, but on the wet carpet it had turned into a sticky paste. Her new mattress and springs were still wrapped in plastic resting on

their sides off to one side of the room. They were likely to
remain there a while longer while things continued to dry
and the carpet order came in. And, of course, the ceiling
repairs still heeded attention.

"Great," Allie muttered. "Just great. Can't win for losing around this place lately." She felt like Scarlett O'Hara
in *Gone With the Wind* as she closed the condo door on
her troubles and started up to Nate's place. She'd worry
about the mess in her place tomorrow for tomorrow was
another day. Or something like that.

Using the spare key Nate had given her, Allie entered
his condo. Man, it smelled good in here. "Honey, I'm
home," she called, getting into the domestic scene. That
ought to scare Nate but good.

"Hey!" Nate called back from the bedroom. "Where've
you been? I was getting worried."

Allie opened the oven door and sniffed. She closed her
eyes in bliss. Meat loaf—and she hadn't had to make it.
"What?" There were blueberry muffins still warm from
baking sitting out on the counter. The box from the mix
was still lying on the countertop next to several blobs of
batter and the mixing bowl and spoon but who cared? She
didn't know many guys who even came that close to
scratch. Certainly no one in her family.

"Hang on," Nate yelled. "I've just got to sign off."

Ah, Allie thought as she broke a piece off a muffin. He's
on his computer. The man was a workaholic. It was no
wonder nothing was getting done on her place. Nate was
so busy trying to get his business up and running, Allie was
amazed he even had time to wash his face in the morning.
She hated to push him. Allie suspected the guy had a case
of chronic sleep deprivation as it was. She knew he was
awake when she fell asleep and she knew he was awake
when she woke up. He was restless during the night as well,

unless she let him hold her. She'd taken to meeting him in the middle of the bed. He seemed to sleep better and it was no great hardship for her. Not at all. But adding to his problems by insisting her apartment take priority would just plain make her feel bad.

"Yum," she said, after popping the muffin chunk into her mouth. "Good." Sighing then, Allie said to herself, "I still can't let things ride like this forever. Sooner or later we've got to address things downstairs. I'll just have to start handling it on my own this weekend. Send them both on errands or something so they don't know what I'm doing and feel they have to help." She wouldn't go too fast, however, Allie decided as she took another nibble of hot muffin. It was nice not having to come home to an empty place and surely walking into a meal hot and ready to go on the table had to be one of life's greatest pleasures.

After an exhausting, frustrating day at work, what could be better than a hot, fragrant meal and a hotter more fragrant guy? Hmm. Maybe when Nate came out, he'd be naked. He was big on naked in his fantasies. Maybe he'd decide to live one. Speculatively, she eyed the bedroom door.

Nate shuffled into the living area, decidedly un-naked, although his feet were bare. Still, he looked pretty good. Nate Parker definitely made Allie's little heart go pitter-patter.

His jeans were old, worn and snug. The seams were frayed, the knees white. His short-sleeved pale blue broadcloth shirt was unbuttoned over a white T-shirt that was soft from many washings. It had shrunk as well, judging from the way it was molded to his chest. His hair was mussed, his beautiful eyes tired and his five-o'clock shadow had gone on to six o'clock, no, make that at least seven.

James Bond he wasn't.

But he certainly did it for her, Allie decided as she studied him objectively.

"Hey," Nate said again. "You get lost on the way home? I was getting worried." He looked around her. "Where's my dad?"

"Your father decided not to come up and no, we didn't get lost, smart aleck. I had to stay after."

Nate kissed her, right on the lips. It was real casual, as if he'd been greeting her after a day of work for years.

Allie was surprised by the casual possessiveness, but what the heck, she slept with the guy, didn't she? She kissed him back.

"Yeah? You were bad? Had to go to the principal's office, huh?"

"Ha-ha. No, it was just my turn to help out with the after-school child care." She eyed Nate speculatively. "But speaking of your father and principals…"

Nate again looked behind her, as though the old man might have suddenly appeared. "What about them? Where *is* my father? He hasn't let a day go by without stopping in here or at my office at least once since he retired. Has he finally gotten to you? You haven't murdered him or anything, have you? He's a pain, I know, but he *is* my father."

Allie rolled her eyes. "No, I didn't murder him. And Ted's a sweetheart." Then she waggled her eyebrows. "In fact, he's such a sweetheart that I think our principal, Mrs. Johnson, is getting kind of sweet on him."

"No way."

"Way. *And*, I think it's mutual."

"No way."

"Way."

"Wow."

"Yeah. Wow."

It was what he wanted. It was what he'd plotted and planned for ever since his dad had retired. Now that it looked like it might be happening, Nate wasn't sure how he felt about it. "But…dinner's all ready."

Allie shrugged. What could she say? The ways of the heart were strange. "And I'm starving. Let's eat."

"Dad's eating with this principal woman?"

"No, he went to the bookstore to get some ideas on a project she asked him to consult on. He was talking about hitting a drive-through, grabbing a hamburger. He's all pumped about helping Mrs. Johnson redo the library. Dinner dates, I suspect, are on the near horizon."

"But I've got all this food—"

It was the perennial complaint of the unappreciated housewife and it made Allie smile. She knew how he felt, having done most of the cooking at home. When her brothers didn't show up because they'd forgotten to mention various after-school activities—which had been legion— she'd definitely felt sorry for herself and unappreciated. "Aw," Allie said, and kissed his rough cheek. "Look at it this way. Nobody has to cook tomorrow night."

"But—"

"Nate, what is the matter with you? Your father's a grown man. He doesn't have to report in. You didn't let either one of us know you were planning a special dinner, after all. I'm sure he'll regret missing it when he finds out, but meanwhile you're going to have to lighten up."

Nate was immediately indignant. Allie just didn't understand, that was all. "Listen, Dad married his high school sweetheart and never looked at another woman. He's a babe out there in what's become a dating jungle." This was too weird. Faced with the reality of his dreams coming true, Nate didn't know if he could handle it. It was…weird. And oddly, Nate felt, well, abandoned. Now that was mortifying.

Allie snorted. "Tarzan was abandoned as a baby in the jungle and he did all right." She picked up a hot pad and took the meat loaf out of the oven. Slitting open the bag of prewashed salad greens, she dumped some into two soup bowls and set them on the table. "Not only did he survive out there, he got Jane as well."

Nate snorted. "Jane was just using him."

"How so?" Allie got forks from the silverware drawer and slapped it shut.

"She probably got her doctoral thesis out of old Tarz, then dumped him a few years later once she had her degree. The movie just leaves that part out."

Allie snorted as she delivered the forks to the table. She began popping the muffins into a basket. "Well, that's certainly cynical and has nothing whatsoever to do with your father and Mrs. Johnson."

Good grief. Nate felt…anxious. And protective. "This woman's obviously all wrong for him."

"How do you know? You've never met her. She's been a widow for several years and is a sweetheart."

"She can't be too bright, now can she? Asking Dad to help remodel the school's library."

"Mrs. Johnson is very bright. She has a master's in education administration. And they were only brainstorming."

This time Nate snorted. "Just wait. He'll decide to save the school money and remodel himself. The building will collapse, you'll all be out of a job and all those inner city kids you bring the light of learning to will have their bulbs go dim, maybe even out."

"All of that? Wow." She waved the muffin basket at him. "You are so mean." Allie set the basket down and pushed him into a chair. She shoved a bowl of salad in front of him. "Eat. You'll feel better."

Nate took the bottle of proffered dressing and dumped some on his lettuce. He stabbed a clump of shredded leaves with his fork. "My father was a champion clerical worker for the phone company. Champion. He won awards for his handling of customer complaints. He has, however, no small or large muscle coordination to speak of and no real experience with the female sharks of the world. None."

Nate waved the speared lettuce leaves at her. "And you'd be just as protective of your father if he started dating, I'm sure."

"No, I wouldn't. He's a grown man. I'd be happy for him."

"Not if he was dating a bimbo." And Nate would check the woman out as soon as possible.

"Mrs. Johnson is not a bimbo! Never mind. You're being ridiculous. I'm not talking about this anymore." She searched her mind for some innocuous topic. "Are the Cubs playing tonight?"

Nate growled something.

Wow, Nate was really in a bad mood if he wouldn't even talk Chicago sports. Allie was determined his poor mood wouldn't get to her. Honestly, the man just about wept when he knew his father was coming over, but look at him now. He was all out of sorts because his fondest wish had come true. Go figure. "The meat loaf is good," she offered. If the perennial losing Cubs weren't a neutral conversation topic, surely ground beef was.

"It would have been moister an hour ago. When I was expecting you guys."

Allie blew out a breath, set her fork down. "All right, that does it. What is your problem? You lose an account or something? Well, it's not my fault, okay?"

She wanted a fight? Fine. Nate would be happy to accommodate her. "I didn't lose an account. I landed one."

"Congratulations."

"Thank you."

"You're welcome."

"You should have called, let me know you were going to be late."

Brittlely, Allie informed him, "Six-thirty is not late. Ten o'clock might qualify as late. Midnight definitely qualifies as late on a weeknight. Six-thirty is not late."

"It is if you're usually home by four-thirty or five," Nate insisted. Allie was in the wrong here and, by God, he was going to make her admit it.

Exasperated, Allie threw at him, "But I'm not home, am I? I'm in someone else's condo. The condo of some guy I didn't even know one week ago. Some guy who I am not only not married to, I am not engaged to, going with or even dating. In short a guy with whom I have no understanding of any sort with and to whom *I do not need to report!*"

Nate was nothing if not stubborn. "Common courtesy and good manners—"

Allie screeched. She actually did. What was it with men that they could never admit they were in the wrong? Her brothers were the same way. Exactly the same. She grabbed her plate and stood. "Okay, you know what? I'm going downstairs for a while."

"Why?" Nate looked confused.

Men. Allie rolled her eyes. "Because I can count on one hand the number of times I've come home to dinner waiting. I tried to make my brothers take their fair turns, I really did. But you know what?"

She didn't wait for his response. Nate guessed it was one of those rhetorical questions women seemed to go in for. Allie stabbed a finger at him. He leaned back, just in case.

"*Their* idea of putting supper on the table was a frozen

pizza. Or hot dogs rolled up in a piece of buttered bread. Canned chunky style soup so they didn't even have to bother adding water. How you scorch soup, I don't know, but they managed.''

Yuck. A hot dog on *buttered* bread? What was wrong with ketchup or mustard? Nate was starting to resent being put in the same category as Allie's siblings, on more levels than one.

''Oh, I knew they were doing it on purpose. Nobody's *that* bad in the kitchen, but I couldn't take it anymore and they won. I pretty much took over the cooking. Oddly enough, I would like to enjoy this meal, I really would. Savor it, you know? Because it's *never freaking happened before!*'' She whisked her plate away from the table. ''I'm going downstairs to enjoy my food, for which I thank you, in peace and quiet. Maybe I'll be back later, but maybe not. If I'm not knee-deep in water I might start sleeping in my own place again.'' She certainly wasn't about to roll back into bed with this clod even if it was platonic. Mostly.

''Allie—''

''And don't start in on good manners and common courtesy again, buster. You want good manners? I'll give you manners. How about the fact that I have said nothing, *nothing* about the fact that there has been no progress whatsoever on fixing up my condo and it's been a week? I ought to call in repair people and just give you the bills, that's what I ought to do. To heck with trying to be thoughtful and understanding and trying to help you save money so your new business doesn't get into trouble. It's not like you appreciate it anyway.''

Oh, now that he resented. ''Yes, I—''

Ruthlessly she cut him right off. ''We wouldn't be having this conversation if you did, Einstein.''

''Oh, now—''

But Allie wasn't finished. "And to heck with being so freaking understanding of your limited free time because you're so invested in your work. Do you hear me? To heck with all that."

And without waiting for a response—another of those rhetorical questions Nate guessed, figuring Allie didn't much care if he'd heard or not—Allie opened the door, walked out of Nate's condo and slammed said door behind her.

Nate stared in blank amazement at the closed door. Well, that had certainly gone well. He didn't think he'd ever had a woman blow up at him before. They usually went out of their way to accommodate him, as a matter of fact.

He still thought she and his dad should have called. Hell, it's not like this was the Dark Ages and she'd be reduced to using cans connected by string. He'd even buy her a cell phone if that's what it took. Working in the inner city, it was downright stupid not to have one. In fact, he'd take care of that tomorrow.

Nate scrubbed his head with a hand. He had some thinking and some figuring out to do and Nate just hated it when that happened. No wonder guys gagged when women wanted them to get in touch with their feelings. Feelings were a pain in the butt.

All right, he shouldn't have jumped on her. She and his dad hadn't known he was planning to surprise them with a good dinner. Maybe he should have told them, but it was tough to surprise people if you told them beforehand. Nate still thought they should have called, but he was going to have to apologize for jumping down her throat.

Damn it, he hated when that happened, but he'd do it if it got Allie over her crankiness. He didn't like it when she was mad at him, which was really weird when you thought about it. Usually he didn't care if a woman was mad at him or not. There were plenty more around to choose from. With Allie, however, he cared and that was damn scary.

Meanwhile, Allie stomped down the stairwell to her own floor, her meat loaf cradled protectively on its plate in her arm. Opening her condo door, she was immediately assailed with the smell of…damp. There was no other way to describe it. She crossed into the living-dining room and opened the balcony terrace doors.

There, that was better.

Deciding to sit on the sofa to eat, she turned back in that direction and barely bit back another screech. "Oh, no!" Allie wailed. "No, no, no!"

Ted had been with her yesterday when she'd found the rain damage. He'd tried to sop up what he could from the carpet with some towels. Towels that she was just now noticing Ted must have unthinkingly dropped on the sofa when he was done.

Allie set her dinner plate on the coffee table and gingerly lifted the wet mass. She slid a hand underneath and felt the cushion's surface. Wet. Throwing her head back, Allie muttered to the heavens, "Why me? Hmm? That's all I want to know. Why me?"

She'd had a half-formed plan to sleep on that sofa tonight now that her front door would close and lock. Allie wished desperately there was enough floor space in the condo to set up a queen-size bed, other than in the moldy bedroom, but there wasn't.

She should have just ordered a twin.

"Well, I didn't," Allie muttered to herself. She felt the sofa cushion one more time. "And it's looking like the sofa is out, too. Darn, I can't *believe* this."

Allie threw the wet towels on the floor—what the heck, the carpet was already wet—and sat on the one dry cushion. Glumly she shoveled meat loaf into her mouth while she considered her life. She'd spent every evening for over a week with Nate, and almost as much time with Ted. It wouldn't have killed her or Ted to pick up the phone. She'd never thought to explain the rotating schedule to Nate.

"I've been living by myself for so long, I'm not used to anybody worrying if I'm an hour or two later than normal getting home."

It was kind of nice. Her dad and brothers worried, of course, but long-distance worrying was different. She was going to have to apologize.

"Shoot."

Allie put her empty dinner plate down on the coffee table and wandered into the bedroom. She looked up. The ceiling seemed to have dried out. A rather large water stain had appeared on the white surface and some of the paint had popped. Flecks of white paint peppered the carpet like fake snow in a Christmas display.

"Wait another few months and this room'll be right in season."

But there didn't seem to be any real plaster damage, Allie thought as she tilted her head a different direction and studied the ceiling clinically.

"Some scraping, a little primer and paint, the carpet should be in any day…I could be back in here by Sunday," she told herself bracingly. Surely then her life would get back to normal. Surely.

"Right," Allie all but snorted. Her life wouldn't know normal if it bit it on the butt lately. Well, she refused to be pessimistic and instead called up Nate's place.

"Hi," she said. "I'm sorry I blew up."

"No," Nate said. "I was out of line. I apologize."

That surprised her. The men of her acquaintance would die before they'd admit to being wrong. "One of us should have called to let you know we'd be later than what you'd think was normal. You had no way of knowing and I'm sorry you worried."

"It's all right. I shouldn't have jumped on you, especially since I didn't call last night when I was delayed."

"Oh, yeah, that's right. I forgot about that."

Damn. And he'd gone and reminded her. What an idiot. Nate cleared his throat. Next time he'd have to think before he opened his big mouth. "And I'm sure your principal is a very nice lady." Although he'd check on that to be positive. "I'm just not used to my father dating. Anyway, I'm sorry."

Okay, they were both sorry, Allie thought. Now what?

Nate cleared his throat again. "Uh, are you coming back up?"

"I'm going to have to," Allie said. "My sofa got wet, um, somebody put wet towels on it."

"In other words, my dad."

"Well…yeah."

Nate sighed, long and deep. "I'm going to go out for a little while," Allie informed him. "Run a few errands. I didn't want you to worry."

"Oh? Where are you going? Do you need me to come along? Carry anything?"

No. Absolutely not. Not only did she need some time by herself to think, there was no way she was going to let Nate or Ted know her plans. Somehow they'd get sabotaged. Allie didn't know how, she just knew they would. "No, I know you've got work to do. I'm just going to look around the linen sections of some of the stores at the mall, get some ideas. You'd be bored. I'll be fine. Really."

Nate rubbed the furrow over his nose. He did have a lot of work to do. There were several contracts nearly at the signing point and he needed to figure out how to give that final little nudge to get the customer to sign on the dotted line.

But how was he supposed to concentrate on work when Allie was out shopping for linens? That was a code word for sheets that went on beds; specifically, the bed Allie would be sleeping on without him. Nate rubbed harder. Man, he had a skull splitter of a headache coming on just thinking about it.

And all he could do was hope to God she wouldn't be sharing that new bed with some other guy. Now there was a mental image that promised to not just split his skull, but splinter it into a million pieces. But, as Allie had righteously pointed out, Nate had no claim on her. They weren't married or engaged. They weren't dating and they didn't have any sort of understanding. He almost snorted. No, they were just living together, sleeping in the same bed, that was all. Still, all he could do was exhort, "Just be careful, okay? When you get back leave anything you can't easily carry in the car and call me. I'll bring it in for you."

Allie agreed, although she had no intention of following through. Instead, she skipped linens altogether and headed to the home improvement store. There, she picked out her very own stepladder, primer, paint for both the ceiling and walls, paint pan, paint roller and a paintbrush. She was almost to the checkout when she turned back and Allie added a couple of drop cloths, a paint scraper, and two relatively inexpensive box floor fans to finish drying out the carpet. Almost in line a second time, Allie reversed directions one more time and splurged on a rug shampooer, which required a jug of rug shampoo and a smaller bottle of upholstery shampoo. Her Visa card just about maxxed, she headed for home.

Worried the whole time about running into Nate in the halls, although what he'd be doing lurking in the hallway, she had no idea, Allie managed to squirrel all her new stuff up into her condo. She set up the ladder and scraped the rest of the loose paint that hadn't already flecked off from the ceiling.

Glancing at the clock, Allie realized it was well after nine. Nate would be getting antsy, as the stores would have all closed, and she didn't want him coming down to check on her. She'd prime tomorrow, paint the next night. Come hell or high water—no, anything but that, she'd prefer hell to more water—Allie would be back in her own place by Sunday.

Then, with the perspective of a little distance, she'd be better able to see where this thing—she hesitated to call what was happening with Nate, a relationship, under the circumstances—was headed.

Sleeping in the same bed with a man could be distorting her perspective, after all.

The weird thing was, Allie was starting to hope it was headed someplace, that the leak in his pipes had been like fate and just maybe, Nate's odd behavior that evening meant he was going in that same direction, too?

Well, she'd have to wait and see, Allie guessed.

The problem was, Allie hated waiting.

Chapter Ten

Allie worked on her apartment in the afternoons before Nate got home. The rug shampooer she'd bought was amazing, working far better than stepping on towels or even a wet vac to get up the water in the living room. By the time she'd sucked up a couple of gallons of water, shampooed the carpet enough times to get all the gooey baking soda out of it, and used the floor fans to complete the drying process, the place smelled great.

"Even better than before."

The sofa cushion covers had only shrunk a bit when she'd washed them and Allie had managed to stuff the cushions, which she'd dried out in the sun on her terrace, back into them.

When no one was looking, she'd primed and painted the ceiling and redone the walls. She'd pushed, pulled and tugged the mattress and springs into the bedroom and let them fall flat on top of the floor Saturday afternoon while Nate took his father to a Cubs game at her encouragement—it hadn't taken much. There were times when Allie

suspected Nate and his father were in no great hurry to get
her place fixed back up, which made absolutely no sense
whatsoever. Surely Nate would like his privacy back. After
all, Allie assumed he didn't have a roommate for a reason.
Then again, who could figure men? At any rate, Allie had
kept tabs on the game with her radio, and there'd been
enough innings left for her to go out and pick up two sets
of queen-size sheets, a bigger blanket, a mattress pad and
a spread. Miracle that it was, she was indeed back in her
own place that Sunday.

"Finally, the gods are smiling on me again," she murmured as she eyed her condo with satisfaction Sunday afternoon. "I'll invite Nate for dinner tonight," she told herself, thinking out loud. "But I'm not wearing a see-through
apron. No way." Not that she had one. Just to be on the
safe side, she called Ted and invited him, as well.

Nate was getting to her. The way a man can get to a
woman.

Allie wasn't blind to his flaws or anything like that, but
he was getting to her.

In all fairness, they had practically lived together, in a
strictly platonic sense, of course. Well, all right, not always
so strictly. There'd been some kissing sessions that seemed
to catch them both by surprise. Nate was probably equally
well aware of *her* flaws—although Allie couldn't imagine
what those would be. She just hoped he was getting stuck
on her, too. One-sided relationships sucked big time.

Nate and Ted were surprised to see the condo back in
shape. They apologized profusely for not pitching in.
"What happened to the paint I spilled on the carpet?" Ted
wanted to know.

"The bigger bed covered it up," Allie said. "And the
new carpet is in. They'll be installing it early next week."

"I'll make plans to be here to let them in for you so you don't have to take time off," Ted said.

"Deal," Allie agreed.

Ted nodded and she served dinner.

There was very little to clean afterward as the men pretty much vacuumed up everything Allie set before them. Nate wanted to talk baseball—it was coming up on the World Series, not that the Cubs would be involved in that this year either—but Ted kept going off on tangents, pointing out little things Allie had done to turn her condo into her own space.

"Girl's got a knack," Ted said.

"Uh-huh. I still think he had another inning in him. His pitches were still in there."

Nate continued to talk baseball for the next few weeks. Allie had learned long ago with her own brothers, it didn't matter if your own team made the play-offs or not. Guys would watch, argue and come up with checkerboard-like betting pools, a dollar a square, winning square takes all. It was definitely a guy time of year.

She continued to see Nate several times a week all through that time, although Ted was less and less available. Apparently Mrs. Johnson was taking up more and more of his time. A fact which still seemed to make Nate uneasy and which he refused to discuss. At any rate, the leaves on the trees turned and fell off, littering the grass and cement areas until finally only the stubborn oaks had any thoroughly browned foliage remaining. The condo association declared any leaves falling now would not be cleaned up until spring. The first hard frost was predicted for that night and Allie was bringing in the potted geraniums off the terrace when she heard the knocking on the door.

"Hey," Nate said when Allie opened it.

"Hay is for horses," Allie responded, "but 'hey' yourself."

"How's it going?"

"Not that great. How about you?"

"Good, goo—what? What's wrong? You sick?" Nate's hand shot out to feel Allie's forehead.

"I'm not sick." But she didn't knock his hand away. "We had to expel two kids today."

"Yeah? How come? They cheat on a test or something?" Nate asked. He didn't take his hand away until he'd slung an arm around Allie's shoulder. He liked touching Allie. "Well, don't worry. They've probably learned their lesson. I sure did."

"We were painting salt clay topical maps of Asia. I caught them trying to slip some brown tempera paint into my coffee."

"What?"

"They were putting paint in my drink."

Nate boggled. "My God. Did you check to see if that kind of paint is toxic or not? Did they have to pump your stomach or anything? You look all right. You probably lucked out. When I was a kid, we used Ex-Lax, but nowadays kids are a lot more sophisticated. My God. It could have been anything."

"That's why Mrs. Johnson expelled them. The mothers didn't understand. Said it was only paint and the label said it was nontoxic. They didn't see what the big deal was."

Nate studied Allie's eyes. "You didn't drink any?"

"No. That's another reason the mothers didn't understand why we were making such a big deal out of it."

"The pupils of your eyes are both the same size."

"I said I didn't drink any. And that only happens with concussions."

"Oh, yeah." Nate cleared his throat, shaken by the size

of the panic that had swept over him when he'd thought she might be injured in any way. "Well, I came down to see if you wanted to pool our resources for dinner. I've got a package of chicken legs upstairs, but you should probably be taking it easy. Put your feet up for a while then come on up in, say, half an hour. I'll have put together something by then."

Allie wanted to spend the evening with Nate. It was weird, but while they'd only been together for not quite two weeks and back in their own places for twice that, she still missed him the nights she didn't see him. "I've got some frozen green beans and a sweet potato. I can—"

"No. You've had a bad day. You need some coddling. Hand them over. I'll take care of everything."

Allie all but sputtered, "Coddling? I don't need—"

"All right. Bad choice of words. *You* may not need it, but I need to do it." And Nate held out his hand imperiously. "Now hand over the beans and the potato, lady, before things get rough in here." He tried for a mean look, but Allie knew him too well by now and it just didn't work.

She thought about that.

You know, if her brothers had tried that, they'd get a good swift kick in the shins. With her brothers, she'd felt smothered. But with Nate, it was sweet. She *did* feel coddled and she liked it. Go figure. Allie handed over the frozen veggies and the sweet potato.

Nate kissed her on the forehead. "See you in a few." And took off.

Man, she was mush when he did stuff like that, although she liked it better when he hit her mouth with his lips. The good news was he was doing that kind of thing, especially the lips on lips rather than forehead thing more and more frequently. Allie took a cake mix down and read the directions. Cupcakes would bake faster. She went for those. After the past two months, she knew for a fact Nate was partial to yellow or white cake with penuche frosting. She got out the brown sugar and butter.

"You weren't supposed to do anything," Nate said when she appeared with dessert.

"Cupcakes aren't exactly hard work."

Nate eyed them suspiciously, then her with concern. "Even so."

"You don't have to eat them."

"That's okay. I mean, since they're here and all."

That's what she thought. Allie bit back a chuckle.

Nate had baked the chicken legs after slathering them with barbecue sauce. He'd sautéed the beans with some diced onion, the way he'd seen Allie do it. The sweet potato had been microwaved, split into two, then fixed with butter, brown sugar and cinnamon. Nate had even added grape tomatoes and some cucumber slices to the bag of pre-washed salad greens he'd opened. Was he cute or what?

"Wow, you really went all out. What's the occasion?"

"The little juvenile delinquents could have killed you."

"Yeah, well, they need to work on their sneakiness first."

"It's not funny."

Allie sighed. "I know, Nate. I was there, remember? I know."

Nate studied her for a moment. "Sorry." He took a deep breath, expelled it. "Okay, we'll talk about something else. Uh, it's supposed to get really cold tonight. Thanksgiving and then Christmas will be here before you know it."

They talked about inconsequential things while they ate, then Nate offered to put on a movie. "You haven't seen my DVD player yet."

"I don't want to watch a war movie," Allie warned. "Nothing with more than one or two dead people."

"Ha! Got you. I was thinking of you when I picked this one up. ESP or something. It's an old Meg Ryan. *I.Q.* She's Einstein's niece. Not even one dead person."

The movie was funny and cute. Allie and Nate sat cuddled together on his sofa while they laughed. When the movie ended, he used the remote to click everything off. "See?" he said, turning to Allie. "No bodies. Say, 'thank you.' I went in there planning to get the new Arnold Schwarzenegger movie, after all."

Allie shuddered. There'd have been bodies flying every which way. "Thank you," she said, and gave him a light kiss. On the lips. To heck with foreheads.

Or at least it was supposed to have been light. Nate caught her face in his hands and held it while he deepened the kiss. He may have left Arnold behind at the video place, but he was definitely on a raid of his own.

Nate released her long enough to murmur, "You are so damn pretty." Then his mouth was back on hers, hot and open, his tongue seeking entrance. Oh, yes. This was more like it. Allie immediately granted access and his tongue slid in to play with hers. She'd grown accustomed to Nate's kisses, liked them. A whole lot. Nate's arms were around her now. One hand slid under the bottom hem of her sweater. Lightly it played up and down her spine, making her shiver. She felt the clasp on her bra give. "Nate?" she whispered.

"I worry about you, baby. All the time."

"You do?"

"Yeah. You scared me but good tonight."

"Nothing happened, Nate."

"Yeah. I keep telling myself that." His hand slid from her back to the front, gently cradling her breast. His thumb lightly strummed a nipple. "You're so delicate, though. Fragile almost."

That kind of remark with anybody else would have been
good for a smack and a lecture. She was not fragile. Allie
shivered, curled even farther into him. Although, come to
think of it, she was feeling a little breakable tonight. And
Nate was being so gentle, so caring, as though he could
sense her vulnerability.

Allie wound one arm around his neck. The other slipped
under his shirt to play with the light furring of hair on his
chest. She had no idea how it had happened, but God, she
loved this man. Somehow Nate had sneaked under her defenses when she wasn't looking and Allie, well, you could
probably talk around it, dissect it, write a thesis on it, but
it all boiled down to—Allie loved Nate. Was that scary or
what?

Nate left Allie's mouth. He slid his lips down her neck,
nibbled at her neck, letting her feel his teeth a bit. Reaching
behind her, he undid her bra then hiked up her blue cotton
sweater and gazed at her breasts. "Stay with me tonight,
Allie," he murmured. Considering their history, Nate decided to clarify what he wanted from her. "I swear I'll
make it good for you. I've wanted you for so long. It almost
killed me to sleep in the same bed with you and not take
you. Please stay. Let me make love to you."

Oh, Lord. Nate wanted to make love with her. And don't
think she hadn't noted the wording he'd used—make love.
Carefully he nuzzled her breast with his lips, swirled
around the nipple with his tongue a few times before closing his lips around the areola and lightly beginning to
suckle. Allie thought she'd die right then and there. Would
she even live through his lovemaking? Only one way to
find out. She was going to do it. She loved him and she
really was going to do this. Allie opened her mouth—

The downstairs buzzer rang.

Nate was as disoriented as if he were surfacing from a deep sleep. "What? Who?"

The buzzer rang again. Allie wanted to weep.

Nate was just plain mad. "Who the hell? We'll just ignore it." He lowered his head once more.

It rang a third time and Nate swore pungently. Whoever it was had a real death wish.

Allie was already reaching behind to fix her bra. She pulled her sweater down. "You better see who it is." She lifted up and almost killed Nate when she pressed into his lap. "They sound kind of determined."

Yeah. They did. And whoever it was was about to discover the true meaning of pain, because they were going to shortly experience a slow and torturous death. Grumbling, Nate shifted Allie to one side and got up to answer the summons. It was difficult to walk in his state of arousal, but he made it over to the intercom. "Yeah? Make it good."

"Nate, it's Dad. Can I come up? I need to talk to you."

Nate released the button long enough for a bit of inventive swearing. "It has to be right now?" Nate winced as he said the words. But damn it, he really, really did not want to talk to his father at this moment.

"It's kind of important."

Sighing, Nate pushed the door release. His father was his father, after all. And, if there was a God, Ted wouldn't stay long. But maybe Allie would. Till morning at the very least.

Allie rose, running her fingers through her hair and shaking it back into place. "I'll just stay long enough to say hi to Ted then take off, give you two some alone time."

So when had the gods ever smiled on him? He hated whiny crybabies, especially guy whiny crybabies but damned if he didn't feel like weeping. If Nate wasn't careful, he'd find himself blocking the doorway with his body when Allie tried to leave and wouldn't that just be a sight to behold?

Ted arrived and Nate thought he deserved some kind of award for the way he graciously allowed his father in rather than snarling at the poor guy. Ted couldn't have known what he was interrupting, which was all that saved him. "What's up?" Nate asked.

"Hi, Ted," Allie said, kissing the older man's cheek. "Good to see you."

All right, so Allie got the award for graciousness. Unless, of course, she hadn't been as fully involved as Nate had been. Damn, there was a scary thought. He refused to even entertain that nightmarish idea. She had been. She had to have been.

"Allie," Ted said, taking both her hands in his and returning the buss. "I'm glad you're here. You'll want to hear this, too."

Oh, God. Nate instinctively braced. He pulled Allie in closer and threw an arm around her shoulder in an aeons-old instinct to shield while he racked his brain. Ted hadn't attempted to fix anything in Nate's place lately and there hadn't been time for him to somehow gain access to Allie's and do anything too terrible since he'd buzzed him in. Maybe he'd come to inform Nate he had cancer. A malignant brain tumor. Leukemia. Lupus. Something awful. What would he do? "What, Dad?"

Ted shuffled his feet and looked embarrassed. "Your Mrs. Johnson," he said to Allie.

"My Mrs. Johnson? The principal at St. Stephen's? What about her?"

"Well, she's…that is…uh…she's quite a woman, don't you think?"

Allie nodded her agreement. "Yes, I do. She's wonderful."

Now Ted was pleating the fabric of his pants with his fingers. Nate was really getting confused. Okay, so the principal had cancer?

"I asked her to marry me," Ted confessed in a rush. "She said yes."

Both Allie's and Nate's eyes bugged out. "What? What!"

Allie hugged Ted and kissed him. "Ted! That's wonderful. Congratulations! Nate, isn't this great?"

Nate didn't know what to think, he only knew that he felt bad. Sneaky and underhanded, and that was just for starters. Yes, he'd wanted to marry his dad off, but now that he'd pushed him on the path, he felt guilty. "Uh, Dad, you're sure you really want to marry this lady?"

"Yeah, I am. I loved your mother, Nate, lived with her for thirty years, but I'm lonely and Monica is special. Totally different from your mother, but still really special. I don't want to spend the rest of my life alone." Ted shrugged. "I mean, come on, you don't want your old man hanging around all the time. You've got a life of your own. I understand that."

Nate's shoulders hunched. Great. Make him feel even more like a heel.

"And I think I can make Monica happy." Ted straightened his posture. "I'm certainly going to try."

Nate cast about for something to say. "Yeah, but...but...it hasn't been all that long. Do you love her, Dad?"

"Yeah, you know I really think I do. Silly, but I feel like a young buck all over again."

Oh, man. God. Holy cow. Nate swiped a hand over his face. "Uh, Dad? Why don't you sit down for a minute. I kind of need to tell you something."

"Stop acting like there's a death in the family," Allie

hissed as she gave Nate a poke in the ribs with her elbow. "Be happy for him. At least try and fake it."

Happy, yeah, right. As if. Nate took a breath. "Okay, Dad, here's the thing. You know how you took an early retirement and then Mom died? Well, you were kind of lost. All this free time, nothing to fill it. To be honest, you were kind of making me crazy."

Ted nodded. "Yeah. Took me a while, but I got that. That's why I agreed to go to Allie's school with her when you suggested it."

"Yeah, well, I kind of had an ulterior motive there."

"I know, Nate, it's all right."

"No, I wasn't just trying to find something to occupy a little of your time, Dad. I wanted you busy. I mean like twenty-four-seven busy. What can I say?" Nate asked with a shrug to explain the inexplicable. "I was hot under the collar after the fireworks, the bookkeeping, the pipes. I figured the school would maybe have some unattached women. You know, an attractive widow, something like that. Okay, but the main reason I went ahead and pushed you into getting out in the world again? Your matchmaking schemes made me so mad I decided to turn the tables and do the same thing to you. My intentions were to marry you off, get you completely off my back."

Ted nodded agreeably. "Worked."

"Dad, don't you get it? It was a rotten, low-down thing to do. If you marry this woman it will be because I was being sneaky and underhanded. You can't do it. You just can't."

"Watch me. I'll even say thank you. I'm about to be a very happy man for the second time, Nate. I can overlook a lot."

"Dad—"

"All right. Let's try it this way. Think I haven't noticed

how much time you and Allie are spending together? You wouldn't let the fact that you met Allie through me prevent you from marrying her, would you? Throw away a chance at happiness, should you two decide you're right for each other, just to show your old man he couldn't manipulate your life?''

"Uh..."

"Would you?"

"Uh..."

Allie looked at Nate in dawning horror and knew he would. Look at him scrambling to come up with something PC. He absolutely would. He'd asked her to spend the night, this time for real, not just sharing the bed but their bodies as well and it wouldn't have meant a thing to him. Nothing. Her brothers were right. Men had sex, they didn't make love. A woman was a fool if she thought differently. Allie took an instinctive step back.

"Now, Allie," Nate said, having caught the movement out of the corner of his eye.

Allie took another step back toward the door, toward freedom. "Don't you *now Allie* me, you jerk. You had an itch and I was conveniently on hand to scratch it, is that it? That's called *using*, Nate, and it's not very nice. In fact, it's a whole lot lower than the stupid games you and your father have been playing with each other. Her back was right up against the door now, and she was almost free. "When you asked me to spend the night tonight, I thought I was saying yes to a relationship that would be going somewhere, but it's a dead end, isn't it? I should be glad to find out now before I'd invested too heavily in us, but I can't feel anything right now."

"Allie, I—"

Allie reached for the knob she felt in the small of her back and gave it a vicious twist, opening the door. "You know what, Nate? The answer's no. Now and forever, *n-o*. Don't call me anymore, okay? I'm busy. Perpetually busy." She turned to go, then whirled around. "Oh, sorry, Ted. Congratulations. I'm very happy for you and Mrs. J." Allie promptly burst into tears. Then she left. For good.

Nate and Ted stared at the closed door for several seconds in silence. Finally Ted cleared his throat. "I take it my timing was off tonight."

"Just a little," Nate responded grimly. He shoved his hands into his pockets, still contemplating the closed door.

"Uh, aren't you going after her?"

"And tell her what? She's absolutely right. I'd asked her to spend the night when I had no intention of…anything."

Ted gave him a pitying look. "Dumb. Man, talk about cutting off your nose to spite your face."

"Yeah. Talk about."

Ted rubbed his nose as though to check it was still attached. "Well, I'm sure you're relieved to know I don't have time to stick around and rub your face in your stupidity. Monica and I are going out to look at rings." Ted shook his head as he headed for the door. "First keeper he's ever found and what does he do? He throws her back. Go figure."

Nate spent that night and the following day justifying. His reactions had been perfectly understandable. No one wanted a parent picking out their spouse. A man liked to make his own choices, after all. He'd be the first to admit that Allie was bright, cute, personable, a good friend, mature, altruistic, sexy, clean, good mother material yet still totally hot. Under any other circumstances…

Nate rubbed his eyes tiredly. God, he was a fool.

But, what to do?

He had some major sucking up to do, for sure. "I may have inherited Dad's total lack of handyman capabilities," he grumbled, "but at least I got Mom's ability to pick up a phone and call a professional. She's damn lucky, now that I think about it. At least she won't have a lifetime of bursting water pipes and slobbered paint to deal with if she marries me."

Damn, but he missed her. His bed was empty, his condo was empty, even his office where Allie had never even visited felt empty without her.

"I'm pathetic," he said. Nate rose from his chair, circled his desk. "I'm also going to do everything in my power to fix things up. I am *not* stupid." Not once he'd been hit over the head with reality, that was. "I have seen the light. I can do this." He knocked on his partner's open office door. "Jared? I need to talk to you, man."

Once he'd heard the whole story, his partner's opinion was short and pithy. "You are so screwed."

Yeah, looked like. And he was likely to remain in this pitiable condition for a good long while at this rate—like the rest of his life. "Thank you, Jared. That's very helpful. What I need here is a little advice on how to get myself unscrewed."

Jared leaned back in his chair, hands prayerfully clasped at his waist while he studied the ceiling for inspiration for a while. "Okay, women like romantic stuff, you know like flowers. Have you tried flowers? You don't even have to go to a florist anymore. They've got them right at the grocery store now."

Nate crinkled his nose. "Flowers? You really think so? Aren't they, I don't know, like trite?"

"Things become trite because they work," Jared informed him knowledgeably. "It won't hurt to try, anyway."

Nate still wasn't sure, but he was a desperate man. "All right, I'll try them, but no roses. Roses are definitely trite."

"They know you dropped a bundle if you show up with roses," Jared pointed out.

"So I won't send daisies, either. I'll find something exotic. Something that shows I put a little thought into their selection."

"If flowers don't work, try candy," Jared advised.

Nate rolled his eyes. Jeez, it was a miracle the man ever had a date if that was as creative as he could get.

Nate came home the next day to a message on his answering machine. It was a perfunctory sounding thank-you from Allie for the flowers he'd sent. She'd called at a time when she'd known Nate wouldn't be there so she wouldn't have to talk to him, Nate guessed, and he knew he had a job in front of him. "That is one seriously ticked off lady," he told himself, contemplating his next move. Unfortunately, romance and mush were not exactly his forte. They pretty much made him cringe, as a matter of fact. "I'll try the candy before I really get desperate," he decided, although he didn't really hold out much hope. "I'll even go for the good stuff. Fannie Mae. That should make her happy."

Nate rang Allie's doorbell, intent on making the delivery himself this time. No more opportunities for perfunctory answering-machine thank-you's. He buzzed a couple of times and tried knocking, but nobody answered the door. Where the hell was she? It was nine o'clock on a school night. She had to get up early the next morning. She should be home. He knocked once more and the neighbor's door, rather than Allie's, opened.

"Are you looking for Allie?"

No, he just liked banging on random doors. Still, he managed to respond civilly, "Yes. Yes, I am."

"She's not home."

You know, he was starting to get that impression himself.

Nate gritted his teeth. "Would you happen to know where she is, Ms., uh?"

"Klegman," the neighbor helpfully supplied. "Marcy Klegman. And Allie went home."

She was senile. Great. "I thought you just said she wasn't home."

"Home home. To Michigan."

Nate felt a wash of panic. "What about her job? Doesn't she have to work?" She hadn't quit and left for good, had she?

"It's fall break," Mrs. Klegman informed him. "No school for a while."

Great. Just great. He knew approximately where her family lived. They'd talked about her hometown. Nate turned to leave. "Oh, Ms. Klegman, would you care for some Fannie Mae chocolates?" he asked. He just happened to have a box with him.

The whole way up the staircase and long after Nate was back at his own place, he brooded. Looked like any apologizing he'd be doing would be in front of her whole family. Brothers, she'd said. How many? He didn't recall anything more numerically specific, just that she had brothers. Definitely plural. "So at least two. Plus her father. A minimum of three." How big were they? He racked his brain but couldn't remember many details other than the fact they'd all driven her crazy and were wildly overprotective of their only sister. Oh, God. How many broken bones would it take before the males in her life let him talk to her? If she'd told them anything about him, they'd surely be out for blood. Nate just hoped they let him live at all.

Nate straightened his shoulders. Well, Allie deserved her pound of flesh. He was going to see that she got it.

But what to do or say when he got there? How did he

present his case so she'd forgive him? That was the burning question.

"No more flowers," Nate muttered as he paced. "And forget the candy, too. Something special, something unique, just for her." He paced some more, then snapped his fingers. "Fantasies. We talked about those." He'd get her a see-through apron. Where to go for one of those? "No. That was my fantasy. Let me think. What was hers?" He thought until his head was ready to explode. "Sports. It had something to do with sports. I know! She wanted a guy who wouldn't whine or cry foul when she beat him at a game. She's going to have to beat me at something." Man, he'd heard women fantasized about Prince Charming fitting them with a glass shoe and taking them off in a horse-drawn carriage or a white knight carting them away on a white horse. Those would have been mortifying enough. But no, he had to lose at sports to her in front of her brothers, who would no doubt all think he was a wimp.

Well, no point whining. Whining would have him out of the game quicker than losing. What would it be?

He snorted. Anything with a ball. It wasn't that Nate wasn't athletic. He was. He'd lettered in swimming, track and cross-country. He worked out, too, and there was little doubt in his mind he could out press Allie on his worst day. The problem was, he had no depth perception. The surgery and eye exercising and patching had straightened out his eyes, but he still did not have binocular vision. In other words, he couldn't tell exactly where moving things—like balls—were in space, which made it tough to catch them and was a major sore point with Nate. He loved all those games.

"So, what's it going to be?" he asked himself.

He could challenge Allie to a game of horse. That would certainly be humiliating.

Or take her to the batting cages. She could really whomp on him then.

Then there was tennis, racquetball or golf. Lacrosse. Badminton. Volleyball. Gee, there was an entire world of ways for him to look and feel stupid out there. Who'd have thought?

Grimly Nate used the Internet to find her home address and get driving directions, then called Jared and his father to let them know where he'd be and packed a bag. He locked up his condo, climbed into his car, made a quick stop at a Pier One and a longer one at a jewelry store and started to drive.

Four hours later, he found the house and pulled into her driveway.

"What are you doing here?" Allie asked when she answered the door.

At least she hadn't slammed the door in his face. There was good news. "Do you have a basketball?" Nate asked. He'd noticed the crooked hoop hung up over the garage door at the end of the driveway.

Allie looked startled. "You drove all this way to borrow a basketball?"

"Not exactly." Nate cleared his throat and tried to think. It was tough to be suave and debonair while asking for a beating. "Uh, Allison, would you care to join me in a game of horse?"

Allie was beyond startled. She was now staring at him as if he'd lost his mind. "Horse?"

"Yes. Please."

"Horse. The man who I know I told I didn't want to see again drives for hours then wants to play horse. Fine. We'll play horse." Allie threw her arms up in the air and came out the door. "I don't understand any of this, but the ball's in the garage. Come on. This way."

"Um, perchance might any of your brothers be at home?" Might as well make the humiliation complete.

"Perchance?"

What, the woman didn't know courtly when it was right in front of her face? It was probably contradictory to try for knightly while knowing you were about to get stomped into the ground, but damn it, he was doing the best he could. The least Allie could do was appreciate it. Nate nodded regally. "Yes. Perhaps they might enjoy joining us."

"You are acting extremely weird, Nate. And no, they're not here. They are all gainfully employed and even when they're not, they go home to their wives and kids, not here."

"I see." And was greatly, incredibly relieved. Maybe this wouldn't be so bad. "How about your father?"

"He is also gainfully employed and currently at work. I'd ask about your own state of employment, but you couldn't have been fired. You own the company so I sure don't know what you're doing here in the middle of a work-day, but here's the ball." She handed it to him.

Nate took it, dribbled a couple of times, then shot. It hit the backboard, but that was about all you could say for his aim. Allie retrieved the ball, bounced it a bit, then let loose. The ball caught nothing but net. "I didn't call it, so it doesn't have to be a swish," she informed him graciously.

Nate nodded grimly and took the ball, eyeing the basket intently. This had been a bad idea. While he was grateful for the lack of audience, horse still had entirely too many letters. And there was little doubt in his mind he'd pick up every one of them before Allie had even one. He should have suggested something shorter. Like ass. Nate shot the ball. Close, but no cigar.

"That's *h*."

"Yes, I know."

It seemed like forever, but was probably closer to fifteen minutes when Nate picked up his final *e*. Allie tucked the ball under one arm. The two of them eyed each other in silence. "Okay. We played horse. Now what?" she finally asked.

"I'm not whining," Nate said.

"Excuse me?"

"I'm standing here not whining."

"Nate, what are you talking about?"

"You said you wanted a guy who wouldn't sulk or whine if you beat them at something. You won. I'm not whining."

It took a moment for Allie to connect. When she did, she pointed out, "Letting me win doesn't count. You had nothing invested."

That made him mad. Nate ran his hand through his already disheveled hair. He'd let some girl totally whomp on him and this is what he got? Where was the justice? "What are you talking about? I was invested. Totally invested."

"At least my brothers try and it's close. I can only win some of the time. All I had just then was an *h*. When you make it so obvious, it's like condescending. Insulting." Allie crossed her arms over her chest and glared at him.

So he drove four hours to give Allie what she'd said she wanted and this was what he got? Oh, he didn't think so. "I tried," Nate intoned ominously. Not only did he feel unappreciated, he was also starting to feel a little scared. "All right, never mind. Forget it. Let's try something different. Where are the batting cages?"

"Batting cages?"

"You are starting to get on my nerves."

"Oh, well pardon me all to pieces. You want to go to the batting cages, we'll go to the batting cages." Allie returned the basketball to the sports box in the garage and grabbed a couple of baseball bats. "Well, what are you waiting for? Come on." She led the way to the car.

It didn't take long for Allie to realize Nate wasn't play-acting. "You really can't hit the ball, can you?" she asked as another ball whizzed by him.

"Quiet. I'm concentrating." He shouldered the bat, waited for the next pitch.

"All right, keep your eye on the ball. Get ready. Here it comes."

Nate swung, caught enough of the ball to foul it off.

"Better," Allie decided judiciously. "If you—"

Nate turned and glared.

"Just trying to help."

"Don't."

Nate managed to get a few hits. Nothing like what Allie accomplished when it was her turn, however. When they were done, he turned to her, forcing the corners of his mouth up into a parody of a smile. "Look," he said. "Doesn't bother me at all."

"Uh-huh. I can see that."

"Would you like to play tennis now? Racquetball?"

"I don't think so. Your teeth will be ground down to nubs by then."

"I'm fine."

"Sure you are."

Nate gritted his teeth. Not that he'd admit it, but Allie could well be right. "So am I forgiven for being a jerk?"

Allie eyed him speculatively. "I don't know. I'm still not going to sleep with you if we're not going anywhere with this relationship."

"Yeah, I got that before you left. Come on, get in the car. Let's go back to your place."

"What for?"

"You'll see."

The drive back didn't take long. Allie climbed out of the car and said, "Now what? I really don't feel like another game of horse."

"Stand over there," Nate directed, pointing to a spot by the garage under the basketball hoop.

"What for?"

"Just do it, okay?" Nate popped the trunk of his car and pulled out a thick column of wood. He dragged it over to the garage and set it on end. Then he picked Allie up and sat her on it.

"What's this?" she wanted to know. Man, he'd done that easily. She couldn't help but be impressed. The hand-eye coordination might be a bit off, but the biceps were dead-on.

"A plant stand. It was the closest thing I could find to a pedestal. I got it at Pier One on my way out of town." Nate cleared his throat. The time had come and he wanted to get this right. Please, God, let him get it right.

"My mother used to tease my dad about how she was meant to be put on a pedestal and adored, not do housework and stuff. He'd tease her right back that she should have married some rich guy instead of falling for a working stiff like him. Well, I'm not rich, although I have big plans along those lines, but I'm not totally stupid, either. I mean, it might have taken your leaving to make me realize what an idiot I was being, but look, see? Here's your pedestal and I do adore you. You're the best thing that's ever happened to me and I was too darn stubborn to see it."

"Oh, Nate—" Allie reached for him and the plant stand wobbled precariously.

"Whoa, careful there," Nate said, steadying her. He fumbled in his pocket, then knelt in front of the stand. "Allie, if I promise not to whine when we play miniature golf or tennis, will you marry me?'' he asked as he presented a small ring box to her.

"Yes,'' Allie breathed, opening the box and gasping. "Yes.'' It was a large, beautiful pearl, surrounded by small diamonds. "It's beautiful.''

"It kind of reminded me of a ball,'' Nate said. "When you look at it, you can think of all the games you can beat me at.''

She laughed.

"But when we pick a spot for our honeymoon?''

"Yeah?''

"We're going to make sure it has a pool and beach or someplace we can go running.''

Allie smiled. She didn't care where they honeymooned so long as she got to spend the rest of her life with this man. "Why is that?'' she asked.

"Lady, I'm going to swim and run rings around you.''

Then Nate took the box from her, removed the ring and slipped it on her finger. He hugged Allie and they both laughed joyously. Life was going to be good, Allie thought. But they'd just see who ran rings around whom....

*   *   *   *   *

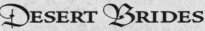

It's romantic comedy with a kick
(in a pair of strappy pink heels)!

Introducing

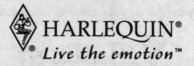

eHARLEQUIN.com

The eHarlequin.com online community is *the* place to share opinions, thoughts and feelings!

- Joining the community is easy, fun and **FREE!**

- Connect with **other romance fans** on our message boards.

- Meet your **favorite authors** without leaving home!

- **Share opinions** on books, movies, celebrities...and *more!*

Here's what our members say:

"I love the friendly and helpful atmosphere filled with support and humor."
—Texanna (eHarlequin.com member)

"Is this the place for me, or what? There is nothing I love more than 'talking' books, especially with fellow readers who are reading the same ones I am."
—Jo Ann (eHarlequin.com member)

Join today by visiting www.eHarlequin.com!

If you enjoyed what you just read,
then we've got an offer you can't resist!

Take 2 bestselling love stories FREE!

Plus get a FREE surprise gift!

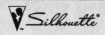

COMING NEXT MONTH

#1684 LOVE, YOUR SECRET ADMIRER—Susan Meier
Marrying the Boss's Daughter

Sarah Morris's makeover turned a few heads—including Matt Burke's, her sexy boss! But Matt's life plan didn't include romance. Tongue-tied and jealous, he tried to help Sarah discover her secret admirer's identity, but would he realize *he'd* been secretly admiring her all along?

#1685 WHAT A WOMAN SHOULD KNOW—Cara Colter

Tally Smith wanted a stable home for her orphaned nephew—and that meant marriage. Enter JD Turner, founder of the "Ain't Getting Married, No Way Never Club"—and Jed's biological father. Tally only thought it fair to give the handsome, confirmed bachelor the first shot at being a daddy…!

#1686 TO KISS A SHEIK—Teresa Southwick
Desert Brides

Heart-wounded single father Sheik Fariq Hassan didn't trust beautiful women, so hired nanny Crystal Rawlins disguised her good looks. While caring for his children, she never counted on Fariq's smoldering glances and knee-weakening embraces. But could he forgive her deceit when he saw the real Crystal?

#1687 WHEN LIGHTNING STRIKES TWICE—Debrah Morris
Soulmates

Joe Mitchum was a thorn in Dr. Mallory Peterson's side—then an accident left his body inhabited by her former love's spirit. Unable to tell Mallory the truth, the new Joe set out to change her animosity to adoration. But if he didn't succeed soon their souls would spend eternity apart….

#1688 RANSOM—Diane Pershing

Between a robbery, a ransom and a renegade cousin, Hallie Fitzgerald didn't have time for Marcus Walcott, the good-looking—good-kissing!—overprotective new police chief. So why was he taking a personal interest in her case? Any why was *she* taking such a personal interest in *him*?!

#1689 THE BRIDAL CHRONICLES—Lissa Manley

Jilted once, Ryan Cavanaugh had no use for wealthy women and no faith in love. But the lovely Anna Sinclair seemed exactly as she appeared—a hardworking wedding dress designer. Could their tender bond break through the wall around Ryan's heart…and survive the truth about Anna's secret identity?